BODY CUTS

Elizabeth Baines was born in South Wales. Her previous novel *The Birth Machine* was published by The Women's Press in 1985. She has written short stories and drama for radio broadcast. She now lives in Manchester.

PANDORA PRESS FICTION

BODY CUTS

Elizabeth Baines

LONDON

I would like to thank North West Arts for financial assistance while I was writing the book.

First published in 1988 by Pandora Press
(Routledge)
11 New Fetter Lane, London EC4P 4EE

Set in Sabon 10/13
by Input Typesetting Ltd, London
and printed in Great Britain
by The Guernsey Press Co. Ltd,
Guernsey, Channel Islands.

British Library Cataloguing in Publication Data

Baines, Elizabeth
  Body cuts.
  I. Title
  823'.914[F]   PR6052.A319/

ISBN 0–86358–225–7

PART I

1

This is the story Bron told me:

That first night, I was on the run.

That night, when no doubt there were women everywhere being purposeful and organised – holding down jobs, setting fire to porn-shops – I'm alone on the run in a strange seaside town.

It's dusk. Up above, the lights of a plane signal in the navy-blue sky. The house I've come to seems deserted. There's rain-soaked cardboard where once there were glass panes in the door; the houses either side are boarded up.

Looking round, I step back, and my feet scraping made me jump.

Since getting off the train I've had the feeling of being followed. The branch-line station was deserted, but hadn't another carriage door banged after mine – again, as before, when I'd got on the train? Whoever they were, alighting behind me, they'd disappeared, like silverfish into the cracked-tiled walls.

Were they lurking, watching as I paused with the ticket-collector because my ticket was meant for a different destination altogether? Did they see me stop, hesitate, outside the station, then cross to the newsagent's with its postcard adverts behind wire? Did they see my yellow hold-all bob away along this road, like the cardboard Day-Glow moon in the Dancing-Class concert when I was a child?

Memories waiting to pounce.

There's a smell in the air: smoke-and-ashes and salt, the old familiar smell of a seaside resort in autumn, summer collapsing back, something burnt out.

Of course, the house must be abandoned: the card in the newsagent's was mottled and old like a brown leaf caught in the wire; ROOM TO LET amongst the others, FRENCH LESSONS, LOST KITTEN, long out of date, no doubt.

So, I've nowhere to go.

But as I make for the gate, my shadow starts, a huge bat on the path: a light has gone on inside the door.

In Hansel and Gretel a witch came to the door. It opens a crack, and a woman's fuzzy head peers. She's suspicious; one woman's closed suspicion for another: it's what I'm resigned to, it's maybe all I deserve.

'Is the room still free?' I ask. My lips are swollen; I'm not sure the words have sounded properly; as if I've lost the power of speech.

But there's the answer: 'Yes,' and the door is opened wider.

I step inside and put my bags down, the yellow hold-all and my small leather case with its corner-reinforcements coming away like torn ears.

I'm being stared at. I brace myself to return the gaze. A thin young woman with bleached hair glistening against the light and a mask of white pan-stick and kohl, dressed up like a landlady in a wrap-around floral pinny.

4

Everyone, anyone could be someone else in disguise. 'One moment,' she says, and she's gone.

Everyone, anyone, can slip away, out of your control, and do things behind your back.

What are the ways of checking up on stray persons? What networks exist for checking up on me?

Brown lino and yellow walls, lit by an unshaded low-wattage bulb; the uncarpeted staircase spiralling up into darkness. Like all those other stairways in places I've lived. I think of my mother suddenly, hissing us quiet on stairs like these, in all those flats our father moved us to before we settled down on the ground without him; she'd bundle us past the tight varnished doors — though half-way down the baby would start yelling anyway, his gulps erupting like comic-strip bubbles out of her arms.

I have the sinking feeling of not having escaped at all.

The voice at my shoulder: 'No key, I'm afraid.'

Explaining then: 'Not for the top room, only the front door.'

She hands me the yale. I take it, but she leaves her hand extended. 'Fifteen pounds a week. In advance.'

Pay up. Truth or dare or forfeit.

I dig in my bag. Her face is shadowed, but I can feel the eyes staring. My panic, and my guilt, fallen back down now like the burnt-out summer, like glowing ash, giving me away.

She leads the way up. My footsteps clonk. Hers are silent, she must have soft soles. A leaking cistern hisses, and through an open dark doorway pale garments float like satirical ghosts.

5

Half-way up, the time-switch gives out. In the sudden darkness, I lose my sense of the rail; I sway, grasping, and inside the case, the thing of Dave's that I've stolen shifts, sounding alive.

Then the light goes on again. She's looking down at me.

What unnerves me is the smile. Friendly or mocking, I don't know which; jailor or fairy godmother I just can't tell.

The room is on its own off a tiny top landing. The air hits you like a cloth, musty and warm with gathered years of rising heat. The ceiling slopes to the floor, bruised by a skylight.

'I'll get you some blankets.'

And then I'm alone.

There are bits of dark heavy furniture adrift on their legs: a single bed, a hard-back chair, a double mattress stored on end, bulging like cold flesh from behind a black-varnished wardrobe; a scuffed chest of drawers with a loose mirror propped on its surface against the wall. My reflection sneaks up from the corner: mouth lop-sided and purple. I pull back my lips to see the gap in my teeth.

I look wicked, unbalanced.

When we were kids, my sister and I, we'd put orange-peel across our teeth and dart to the mirror shrieking, 'That's not me!'

Scaredy-cats, killing ourselves.

Madwoman in the attic.

Is it me?

2

One morning, another autumn long before, the telephone rang.

It was Dave, poverty-stricken artist as he insisted he was, calling long-distance on expensive time, because that was when Boris – my husband, as Dave insisted on calling him – would be out.

The wires pinged. Over the distance, his voice sounded thin.

The day before had been Sunday. He said, 'I planted a rose for you in the garden.'

His garden. His and Amanda's (his wife, as he insisted, perhaps slightly less, on calling her).

Bad taste, I thought, knowing he'd think me prudish. I couldn't feel flattered or consoled; it was too sad and too ridiculous: married adulterers dealing in the clichéd symbols of romance, I would rather keep it light. I laughed. I said, 'What, you mean a memorial? I'm not even dead!'

He went serious. It was as if he himself were ignoring something tasteless. 'It's your colour, it's red.'

'Actually, I rather like yellow in roses.'

'I mean it's the colour that reminds me of you.'

He added, 'I'm keeping you alive.'

I almost laughed. We had another game, my sister and I, we called it *Burial or Cremation*; if you lost you got cremation, because cremation seemed so awful, becoming dust that could just be blown about by the wind; to win was to get burial, we liked that idea better: a good solid headstone and your actual white bones in the warm firm ground: something to show for it; a kind of glory, it seemed.

I thought of telling him, but I didn't.

Don't joke about death, and don't ever cry. Two of the rules with Dave. He often said there were no rules, but that was usually when he was busy flouting somebody else's.

'There are no rules,' he said, wiping his mouth, as I tried to talk to him about the way we were hurting Boris. He said, 'Don't be Puritan and bourgeois,' introducing a rule or two after all. And: 'You're not going to cry, are you?'

He called the waiter, waving his large hand, and had a little guessing game about the piquant ingredient in the salad dressing. He was an expert on food.

It turned out to be mustard, plain old English mustard.

'The best tricks are the simplest,' he said.

Footsteps coming up again. She brings the blankets, thin but heavy and coarse, like blankets from war-time.

'Do you want to put some things in the kitchen?'

Shared kitchen, said the ad. You come prepared, you bring your own food, your own packet of tea, which you keep in your allocated bit of the communal space. I couldn't do that: know so clearly where I end and others begin. I shake my head.

She takes pity. 'Are you hungry?'

Don't look vulnerable. Let the truth out, and all the bits of you will fly away with it . . .

But pity is debilitating. I give in, I nod.

I follow, like a child. The kitchen's a jumble of unwashed dishes and half-opened packets. I move papers off the chair and on to the table. She brings me someone else's left-over bread.

I chew slowly, it's painful to eat.

The grey eyes stare.

'So what's your job?'

(Meaning: How did you get in this state, what's been happening to you?)

I lower my head. I busy myself pretending the papers are still in my way. One's an ad for a local theatre revue, the artwork too bitty, too diffuse.

'Acting,' I say, lying compulsively, but in a way also telling the truth – I've never known who I am, it seems I've been trying out parts all my life.

And there it is: the past, jumping up like a devil from my throat. Boris was an actor.

'Oh. We often get actors staying here.'

Actors go anywhere, actors know everyone. They're trained to do anything.

On the landing, beyond the half-open door, the light clicks off. Actors are trained to walk in the dark.

3

It always troubled me to have to say what I did.

In the circles I moved in – or rather, could have moved in, but mostly kept out of – what you did had to be glamorous and self-enhancing and at the same time of great and lasting use to society. Thus Boris, as an actor into agit-prop and Marxist interpretations of the Classics, Did Something, as they said, with his life. Waitressing and shop-work, of which I had my fair share, didn't count. As for the paintings I did on the quiet, well, I found it best in the end to keep them that way. After all, as Boris would have said if he'd known about them, you couldn't exactly have called them socially useful. Boris on the contrary could congratulate himself that his art was public and dynamic – when he got the parts, that is. A theatre *worker* was how he described himself, scorning the term *artist* as bourgeois individualism.

Once I started working for publishers he conceded me a certain claim: after all, I had a label, *illustrator*, which he couldn't deny, and there was proof, my work in other people's books. Yet there was always that rider: *freelance*. Badge of independence, badge of insecurity.

Freelance, but professional. Dave's ironic compliment in bed.

This was how I met Dave:
I'd illustrated the cover of an anthology on the theme of Extra-Terrestrial Experience, a set of pretty unbelievable anecdotes parading as factual accounts. The contributors were well known and exclusively male, and their pieces tended to run: *An attractive brunette who visited my apartment once . . .*; *A red-headed au pair we had when I was a teenage boy . . .* etc. Boris reckoned it all a plot on the part of Communist infiltrators into publishing to show up these Great Men for what they really were. Boris was an innocent, he underestimated

10

the casual urbanity of the Oxbridge classes, he made the mistake of believing they were as desperately afraid of losing their power as he was desperately anxious to destroy it, and so saw them as vulnerable, and expected the revolution to happen at any time.

I replied, working away at the preliminary sketches, 'Even if ordinary people could be made to see them for what they are, do you think they would care?'

He stopped in the middle of sawing himself a slice of bread, one jeaned leg propped on a stool.

He said, 'I note your terminology. "Ordinary people" indeed. Who, may I ask, are they? And let us examine your assumption of apathy and lack of wit on the part of the populace.'

He jammed a banana between two slices.

'Once again, Bronwen, you expose your true nature as a bona fide child of an Imperialist hierarchical culture.'

He nodded towards the proofs. 'The right job for you, obviously.'

'Quite remarkable,' he added, 'in someone quite so working class.'

Boris had great faith in the moral purity of the working class (his own); he considered me an aberration.

I didn't answer, I was preoccupied, getting the nose right on a portrait of one of the writers which I was doing from a photo; the art editor wanted what he called 'The Face of Fame on the Front'.

In spite of Boris, who always tempted you to side with the enemy, the cover turned out too satirical. The portraits were on the side of caricature, and grouped so as to imply I felt the authors' heads should be knocked together; and placing scenes from the stories (*The Outer Being Who Phoned*, etc.) in thought-bubbles over them was after all much too jokey. I should have known the authors wouldn't like it, and it was of course a mistake to accept the invitation to the publication party – I guess I only went to prove to Boris he couldn't stand his ideological objections in my way.

What most offended was the implication that the experiences recounted had been the authors' own, whereas, it had to be admitted, they were carefully identified in the writing as those of people with whom the authors claimed to have been acquainted. As it was, I'd made the authors out to be a bunch of hallucinating neurotics. There was one thing, after all, that could ruffle these Great Men: any insult to their masculine dignity.

I skulked around for a while, in my plain black dress discreet as a librarian, but when an author moaned to me expecting sympathy, I jumped involuntarily, like a caterpillar from a skin, and gave myself away.

'Oh, you're the artist,' he said, recoiling, and then stiffly, sharpening his face and looking even more like a ferret:

'You've caricatured us as animals. Do I take it you're a feminist?'

As a matter of fact, as a feminist I felt a fraud. It was the end of the seventies, almost ten years into the Women's Movement, and real feminists had given up wearing eyeshadow and high heels and living lives cut off from other women. Looking round the room now, though, at the porcine male paunches and listening to

12

the territorial bark of male conversation, I did feel a great surge of solidarity with feminists. Generally, however, I had a certain philosophical confusion: was it that men had been turned into pigs because of the advantages that society gave them, or had their piggishness, being innate, led them to grab the advantage? A true feminist, I felt, if she didn't actually know the answer, would at least know the terms for discussing it.

At that moment Dave came up, he'd overheard and joined in. He surprised me by taking my side. It gave him a chance to laugh at the ferret-man's expense.

Dave was the author I'd drawn to look like a rat, but now, viewing him in life, I saw he'd be better as a coypu, he was big, with a wide soft face and a large rounded head. I remembered that his story had been rather better than the rest, featuring a farming family troubled by things landing in their fields at night and leaving holes in the ground, and after each visitation the death of another member of the family, who would experience, in the moment of dying, a beckoning manifestation — a fairly competent amalgam of traditional ghost-tale and science-fiction, I thought, with a nicely-placed hint of religious conversion, and the only piece in which the suspension of disbelief wasn't broken by strenuous claims of truth.

Scowling, the ferret-man went away.

Dave turned to me. 'You're left-handed.'

I almost jumped, the way I used to: *Bronwen, hold your pen properly! . . . Bronwen, MUST you slant your paper on the desk that way?*

But how did he know? I was holding my glass in my right hand.

I looked down quickly, ready to believe my senses were deceiving me.

He said, noticing and smirking: 'I can tell from the drawing. Everything in it is being held left-handed. Look.' He picked up the cover and showed me. He was right.

Caught out, caught up on a fish-hook. As if by an almost supernatural power.

4

For this pokey little room, even for a night or two, it seems, I have to have a rent book. Bureaucracy in the slums, red tape amongst the pin-money landladies; there's no escape.

She's gone to get it, and I'm alone amongst the sauce-bottles, in the kind of place where the police, on the look-out for terrorists or student peace-campaigners, might plant bugs. I eye the ceiling-rose and window-frames, and try to think of a name.

You'd think by now I'd be used to false names. First the married one: I woke up wearing it one morning like a glove too tight ever to take off again. Then the name I used for painting, the one that always stayed secret. Come to think of it, it was *Boris*, that was the only false name I grew to accept without thinking.

Suddenly the floral pinny is back in the doorway.

'What's your name?' she asks, pen poised to write it on the book, picking up my thoughts as if by radar, and I jump, more guilty and confused than if caught by surprise, and say without helping:

'Bronwen O'Donald.'

The name I began with: it's so long since I've used it, it's the strangest name of all.

5

I prop a chair against my door. An action, a part prepared for me in every second-rate film or cheap comic-strip. I don't undress. I feel the need to be ready for anything, to be decent in bed, as my mother used to say. She was thinking of fires, and even with your house gone, seeking approval for the cut of your nightie.

There's no bedside lamp. I turn the light off at the door and grope my way back to the bed. I'm almost there when something trips me: the leather case. I hear it hiss as it slips on the nylon pile. I kick it out of the way, and with a thud it hits the skirting under the bed. Good. Let it stay there, with its contents belonging to Dave.

I climb in under the hairy blankets. Through the uncurtained window orange street-light enters like the glow from a burnt landscape. On the wall, the bulging sides of the mattress loom pale, like dead flesh.

I pull the blankets tighter. I am lying in my hairshirt,

15

waiting for the bad times to be over, swaddled like a mummy in the hope of a new and higher life.

I've dropped off, but I'm wide awake abruptly. I lie listening. All at once a yellow crucifix lights up in the air at my side. No: the cracks in the door, not close, but over the room: someone has put the stairway light on.

No sound at all. Eventually the cross blinks itself out. Quietness drops through the house like invisible ink. And then suddenly, in spite of everything, I'm filled with longing, though I don't know for what, or for whom. Is it Dave? Could it be Boris? Do I wish that Boris would come bounding up those stairs, three at a time, a Marxist knight in leather armour, a Desperate Dan? He'd burst in and smash the chair so all the bits of it would go flying, he'd plant his legs wide against the light, and he'd say, because he had a snobbish love of squalor, 'Hey, Bron, this is great!', and he'd have a bottle of Bull's Blood under his arm, and he'd say, 'Let's celebrate!' meaning both sex and opening the bottle, he didn't see a lot of difference, and he'd start undoing his buckle, and I'd see the soft belly-flesh through the holes in his vest, and I'd — what? What would I do now, if Boris really came? How would I feel?

There's a creak outside the door. Boris as a rapist. Boris in league with the CIA. Anyone can be anything, everyone has a flip-side, and every story has more than one possible ending, like a fork in the road or a devil's tail.

16

6

When I first met Boris I'd never have guessed how he'd turn out. In the beginning I didn't notice him, but then one day I almost tripped over him. He'd been making towards me below the university in a tweedy jacket that blended with the bleached end-of-winter surroundings, and then suddenly he was standing in my way.

He shuffled, trying to move aside, and then said, stupidly, 'Hi,' as if he knew me well, which he didn't.

After that he kept appearing, like one of those flecks you get floating in your eye. I'd go into a lecture, and there he'd be, already seated, hunched over his notes, a conscientious philosophy student – this was in the days before he donned the robe of revolution and made insolent late entrances everywhere. It was the time when people – those few who bothered to know him – knew him by his real name, Archie P. Hawfield.

One day, at the end of a lecture, he waited and asked me to go for a drink. He clearly needed to pluck up courage, and the sound of his own voice echoing in the corridor as he called me made him jump.

I went, out of pity, out of callous amusement, out of a sense of my own generous superiority. I have made some mistaken assumptions in my time.

He led the way into a pub where all around there were lamps with blobs of wax squirming in liquid like some kind of sub-life. He sat in the corner and took a tentative swig of beer. In those days of Cliff Richard quiffs, he wore his hair parted and flattened, and had leather patches on his elbows. He looked like a small-town bachelor who lived with his mother.

There was a lamp on the shelf directly above his head. The nodule of wax began to nose its way upwards.

He coughed. He said, 'Er, actually, I do a spot of scribbling.'

Oh God, I thought, he writes embarrassing poems and he wants to show me. The kind of person, obviously, who was so nervous of conversation that he overdid it and directly poured out the secrets of his soul.

I said nothing, instead I enjoyed being cruel, I didn't ask any interested flattering questions.

He coughed again, he went red.

The blob of wax became a bobble on a wavering neck.

And then he blurted it out: in fact, he'd written a play. And having said it, he swelled with pride, and seemed to recover somewhat, and said with a ridiculously overdone air of generosity that I could read it if I liked – why didn't I come round: he'd get some others, we'd do a reading.

He said, 'I've got a part, actually, that would suit you down to the ground.'

I couldn't help it, I laughed; though in fact I felt sorry for him having to work so hard to compensate for nervousness.

Which of course was the trouble: a timid man more than any needs to demonstrate his power.

For weeks he hung around, emerging like a sandfly from out of the surroundings, turning up all the time at my elbow with the dingey, dog-eared manuscript.

It was a relief when he went off early for the Easter

18

vac to do some course at some stage school, though also a surprise: he'd won the place with the play.

7

I'd learnt when my father left that life was simpler without men. I couldn't see any way why all those school-camper types with briefcases were worth getting steamed up about, and there was no point living in hope for the mythologically romantic-poetic sort; yet even women like my room-mate Margaret, a homely body, allowed thoughts of men to dominate their lives.

With Margaret it was fear, of a certain kind.

'They say there's a flasher in the lane above Hall,' she'd say, her eyes wide as she got ready for Methodist Union, tying her scarf with the Eiffel towers beneath her chin. 'Won't you come with me?'

I said I was busy, I didn't like to say religion was another thing I'd put behind me.

'Oh, I don't think I'll go, then,' she'd say.

But she went.

And two hours later she'd come back, red in the face and gasping, 'I ran all the way, I daren't stop in case I saw him!' and in the shine of her eyes there was something not too far removed from thrill.

Then one evening she came back and stood in the doorway quite pale and still. I thought the minister must have snubbed her, or perhaps she'd got left out of organising the showing of the Billy Graham film. She didn't bother to shut the door, she walked across the room and sat slowly down on her bed. I saw then she was trembling.

'What's wrong?'

'The flasher. He came out of the archway at the top of the steps. I couldn't get past, he was right in my way.'

I made her cocoa. I said, 'Look. He didn't rape you. Flashers don't. That's the point. From what I understand, they can't. The whole thing is, they're pathetic.'

I didn't have much sympathy, I felt she'd wished it on herself. Surely what she should have done when the silly bugger stood there with his dilly-dangler hanging, as my Gran used to call it, was have a good laugh. I felt like laughing myself. It occurred to me then to wonder if it was erect, though, and curiosity took over, and I asked. 'What was it like?' and I never found out because Margaret burst into tears.

It was reactions like hers which encouraged it in the first place, I thought uncharitably. Though, after a while, when it was clear that Margaret would no longer go out alone at night, I began to see that it wasn't a matter for laughing.

It was confusing: in my experience, what was sinister was not when men showed things, but when they hid them.

Though then again, in Biology at school I'd preferred to think of Mendel the monk geneticist pollinating peas in a medieval habit: that way you didn't have to think of his man's face and hands.

Then one evening in late April I was coming back from

the library. I heard a sound, a click, beyond the archway – a flick-knife or a gun, I thought, before I knew it was a zip, so that before I could place him as the flasher, and thus pathetic, I was well and truly frightened after all.

Perhaps what happened then was the result of sheer relief. Or sheer surprise. The man coming towards me hadn't been undoing a zip, but doing one up: he was wandering towards me fastening a long loose jacket against the cooling evening air. His hair was lifted by the breeze, hair long and untamed, the way as far as I knew hair hadn't been worn since the previous century. He looked like a poet.

Before he reached me I was in love.

And it wasn't until he did that I realised he was Archie P. Hawfield.

8

Perhaps it was the discovery that changes in men could be for the better. Of course Archie'd had training, at stage school he'd learned how to carry himself and how to dress, but I imagined it was usual to show some potential beforehand. It was more like the emergence of a completely hidden self.

After that, I bucked up my ideas. I cheered up, I began to see jokes where I'd seen none before, I saw the point of real life, as opposed to life between the pages of philosophy books, I thought what a po-faced reductive misery-guts I'd been. And I set out to be rid of that symbol of what I now saw as my total lack of courage – I set out to lose my virginity.

We sat down, Boris and I – or rather Archie, though already I didn't think of him as Archie, already he needed some more exotic name – on the dry dappled leaves in a wood. He didn't seem in any way awkward or shy, or surprised at my taking up with him after all; it was as if his former self had no relevance, and this new self of his and I had all along been in waiting and conspiring together. He was surprised, though, when I pushed him down on the leaves, eager as I was to set the seal on my new approach to life – and consumed with lust besides, at the sight of his slim and bony ankle.

It hardly hurt, and there wasn't any blood. Another novelists' lie exposed – not that I felt so censorious any more towards novelists, or anyone, I had no room now to be interested in anything much outside myself, and certainly had no time to work.

'What about the exams?' I said, though not with any great sincerity, rather to relish my reversal, my new insight that to fail to study for an all-consuming other purpose was not so much self-sacrifice as getting things in proportion.

'Exams,' responded Boris, brushing leaves from his hair with a wonderfully bony wrist, 'are the iceberg tip of a punitive education system that aims to trip people up rather than encourage. As such they should never be taken seriously by any intelligent person.' And he opened a can of beer, and threw the ring-pull over his shoulder, about which I worried for a moment, but then decided it didn't matter, what was one bit of rusty rubbish, when the gesture it had been thrown by was a snook at the whole of the bourgeois world? I must lose my bourgeois inhibitions. Also, I ought to cool it and stop worrying about snakes in the grass behind us. Also, I was preoccupied with a feeling in my lower abdomen like the vibrations of a church organ.

We both only just scraped through the exams. And then it was time for female students to be turfed out of Hall, where university regulations decreed we must live, like boarding-school girls for the hols. Male students, on the contrary, arranged their own accommodation and fended for themselves – in a society where it was still expected that adult men should be cooked and cleaned for, and women should be doing the cooking and cleaning for them, the university authorities obtusely gave the wrong people the practice.

Boris had a flat, and didn't need to go home. He said, 'Stay with me. We could get summer jobs here and work together on a play.'

I really wanted to, but already, at the thought of home, my mother had begun to force herself back into my consciousness: lonely and quiet all day in that little terraced blackened-brick house in the Midlands, soon to be abandoned a third time, when my sister went to college, left all alone with my little brother, her last dependent child; I imagined her, standing at the sink, looking at me coming through the door with my suitcase where once I would come out of breath, having found an excuse to get out of school and check that things were all right at home. I knew I had to go.

Yet I resented it, I felt resentful towards my mother

for making me feel guilty, guilty about wanting to spend my time with a man.

I went home. Once I got there I had no time for her; it struck me I was pregnant.

'No!' I snapped irritably, as she tried to press on me a slice of Victoria sponge, and dashed off in desperate hope to the bathroom. Nothing: time after time, the crotch of my pants swung into view stark reproachful white.

In the garden the apples were beginning to form on the trees, bitter green stems reddening and swelling, and in my body, it seemed, a sharp white pip taking root. And its tentacles would grow, and lock me down in loss and drudgery, like the girl at school who'd had to leave, like my mother.

I lay in bed and did some savage mental imagery: a white maggot-thing, which I skewered with pins of hatred so it wriggled and jerked, flicking up its tail.

Though I must say it troubled me to take the image too far: to see myself as a maggot in the life of my mother.

When my period came, if I hadn't long ago given up religion, I'd have taken it as a miracle, and the whole episode as a sign from God: as it was, I took it more prosaically as an all too worldly sign of my need to be more in control.

And so vowed to have nothing once more to do with men.

Trouble was, when I got off the train in October, there was one standing at the bottom of the stairs looking

24

tall and exotic in a Russian-looking officer's coat. He clicked his heels, and I noticed his long eyelashes, and knew it was Boris.

I said, 'I thought I was pregnant.'

I shouldn't have been smiling.

He grinned. It was his poise and skill I was in love with, his mastery of constant new selves.

He said, 'It's OK, I'm prepared now.' And patted his chest in the place where officers keep a gun.

He got out the rubber. There was a hiatus, which was embarrassing. No more melting into each other out of lustful subversive fervour; you had to think about mechanics. I had to look at Boris's penis, and it was a pity it made me think of the sneaky little flasher. When he snapped the rubber on, I flinched like I did when boys snapped rubber bands at school.

But straightaway Boris became a dab-hand, whisking it on before I knew so I didn't have to look, another skill of his new self, he seemed to prove there was nothing you couldn't overcome.

The woods got cold, and Boris and I consequently became connoisseurs of sex in unusual and dangerous places, one of which was his armchair pushed up against his unlockable door that his flatmates at any time might barge through. We could have used the bed and let them enter and politely back out again, or even warn them beforehand, but our Puritan background, as Dave would have said, would never have allowed it, and anyway we'd got hooked on the excitements of haste and half-dress, and Boris's leather flying-jacket

25

squeaking, creating the feeling of being in a cockpit of a plane on automatic pilot; in spite of our revolutionary pretensions, we would never have been at home in the laid-back flower-power sexual age.

Afterwards we'd sit by his gas-fire and he'd eat his favourite food, which was toast with peanut butter and currants, he had a special ritual he refused to abandon in spite of the unpleasantness of an increasingly sticky floor. He once said it was making up for a deprived childhood – all his infancy he'd longed for this particular recipe, but his mother, believing that currants would give him liquid-paraffin poisoning and that in peanut butter there was something carcinogenic, had always refused it; apparently, the death of his father while Boris was an infant had left Boris's mother neurotic about his health, and a concern with Health Foods was forever more in his eyes a symptom of the neurotic bourgeoisie.

He told me this through great mouthfuls, while beige greasy currants dropped off the toast with a sound like bullets onto the plate. I didn't know whether to believe him, I just laughed and avoided asking any questions, choosing to take it as a big fantastic joke. I felt somewhat that he'd made a mistake, a breach of trust, in referring to the past, and was relieved when he didn't do it again. I didn't want then to know about his father or mother, and I certainly didn't feel like discussing mine.

I liked to think we'd given birth to ourselves.

It was round about this time he got the name of Boris. His officer's coat was the costume he'd acquired for his role as a Russian defector in the current Dramatic Society production. He began to take method-acting to extremes, wearing his coat all day, even indoors, and strutting around darkly and swinging off steps to practise for the jump in a balcony scene. The name stuck, and only Margaret my room-mate didn't use it; irritatingly, she always called him Yorick.

9

It was by mistake, by default, that Boris and I got married.

One morning towards the end of the final year, Margaret and I were woken by a hooting on the road below our room.

I sat up and was momentarily shocked by black smudges on my pillow, thinking they must have come from my ears or my nose, and then realised it was the powder I'd brushed into my hair the night before. With my new adventurous attitude, I'd taken to experimenting with my appearance – though nothing permanent, I liked to have an escape-route – and this particular easy-brush-out powder had turned mysteriously overnight from pale silver to charcoal grey.

'Makes you wonder what's in it,' said Naggy-Maggy, as Boris called her behind her back. I threw her an evil look. She made that kind of spoil-sport remark about everything, all toiletries and foods; whatever you put

27

between your lips or under your armpits, she'd have heard about its unpalatable origins, and insist on telling you precisely what poisons they'd used to dry or distil it, how many bits of heavy metal it had been through or over, or how many times it was likely to have dropped on a cockroach-infested floor. She was full of threats about the environment: every time you poised your finger on an aerosol can she'd tell you off, she had a paranoid notion that every little puff would make the final difference to the whole wide world. She was a real drag. A witch of doom. Boris said it was the one way she had found to make herself important.

One term she came back and she'd joined something called the Friends of the Earth, which I supposed were some branch of Quakers. She said, 'Don't you ever read the papers?' and I scoffed, she knew damn well I'd never do such a boring middle-class type of thing. Boris said, 'This proves it, she's suffering delusions of grandeur, poor round fat thing, she's got no friends of her own, so she thinks she'll be the friend of the round fat world.'

The car-horn was still going on outside, and Maggy said, 'That constitutes environmental pollution.'

We twitched back the curtains and were most surprised to see Boris sitting in a white MG with the hood down, his jaw turning jagged circles as he chewed gum, leaning back with his hands behind his head and pressing the hooter with his heel.

'I didn't know he could drive,' I said, and other women's heads poked out of windows beneath us, and the warden crossed the gravel, her legs punching out beneath her pencil-skirt, to tell him off.

He caught sight of me, and made wild swooping

28

gestures, as if suggesting I jump from the window into the car. I ducked back and dressed and ran down, grabbing my mail from the pigeon-hole as I passed, one letter from my mother in the most economical, nasty brown envelope, which I shoved unopened in my pocket, and then ran outside.

He turned the key in the engine the minute he saw me, and the car was already moving as I jumped in.

'Whose car?' I asked, looking along the bonnet, which wasn't rusty enough to belong to a student.

He tapped his nose with his finger, which was of course when I should have guessed, but I was thinking how sexy he looked doing that – like a gypsy, I thought, or a South American conspirator, and he pressed the accelerator and drove on.

It was another new side to him. And he didn't need maps, he seemed to have an instinct for directions, as we gobbled up the green-and-white glittering countryside.

'Where are we going?' I asked, and he tapped his nose again, but then added excitely, 'To the seaside', and began to sing something about loving California which he said was by a group called the Beach Boys.

I hadn't been driving in the country for years. I was rather shocked by the messes of roadworks we kept coming across, and raw industrial estates I'd somehow never noticed from the train, as though while I'd been growing up, behind my back, the country had changed, and stopped being proper country, but we drove fast enough not to have to dwell on what we saw.

When we stopped for coffee at eleven I opened up my letter:

Dear Bronwen, Just a little note of encouragement as I'm sure this finds you working very hard. Don't overdo it, I know this is a tendency of yours. Remember, all work and no play makes Jack a dull boy.

Since I wasn't a boy anyway, I didn't see why she thought her advice was relevant, but I took it anyway and had a good wheeze, stopping off at a gift-shop and dressing up, since no one here knew me, as a tarty tripper.

'Wow,' said Boris, 'I've always wanted to fuck a girl in a shocking-pink headscarf and shades.' (I had perched some large sun-specs over my own.) We were on the Ferris Wheel at the time, and Boris had set himself the feat of trying to get my bra off before we swung to the bottom again, and we squirmed and giggled, and something slipped half-out of his pocket, and I saw it was a spoon from the cafe where we'd stopped. Which was another moment when I should have guessed about the car.

'I've always wanted to fuck a girl with blood-coloured nails,' he said, looking at the ones I'd painted; I squealed and giggled, I took him as playing a parody of a lustful soulless villain, I never thought that one day I would think of those words again.

'Why did you nick that tatty spoon?' I asked, as we lay behind a breakwater. 'I'm sure you didn't need it.'

'Principle,' he said. 'Removing from the capitalists what isn't rightly theirs.'

At that moment a child looked over the breakwater and solemnly stared.

'Want a spoon?' said Boris, quickly covering his genitals, but the child looked insulted at this presumption of the need for a lesson in subversion, and dropped a cold strand of seaweed on Boris's stomach and ran away.

Before we neared the university again after dark, Boris turned off and drove over a flattened fence and down a track at the side of a field. It was trespassing, of course, and that was the excitement: driving and fucking on the land of the territorial puritan capitalists. We had both got our pants off, and the car had slumped into a rut, when I noticed a light across the field. It divided like an amoeba and became the headlights of a car slowly moving towards us. I had begun to relish with excited fear the prospect of Boris's satirical encounter with an offended blustering farmer, when the headlights dipped, and the moon came out from behind a cloud, and showed up the field as an MOD airstrip, and the vehicle slowly approaching as a police car.

'Shit!' said Boris, and pulled his jeans on double-quick, and threw himself over from the back into the driving-seat, and started revving like mad to get the wheels free. At last we jolted forward, and bounced along the track and shot into the road. Looking round, I saw that the police car had accelerated.

They caught us up in a quarter of a mile, where the main street of the town began.

The cops got out and walked round. Boris was frantically doing up the zip of his jeans. There was no end to the things we could be arrested for – indecent exposure, loitering, resisting arrest, no doubt, maybe something much worse, since we'd been on MOD land. And driving without a licence, I thought, suddenly knowing the truth of Boris's actions: and stealing a car.

'Now then Sonny,' said one of them nastily, 'how come you drove past a sign warning you if you did you'd be breaching the Official Secrets Act?'

I was panicking, I was sure any minute Boris would explode at being called Sonny. The policeman was looking pointedly at his newly-zipped fly. I knew that if we were to seem innocent of trespass and car theft, we had first to seem innocent of sexual immorality. I cast my eyes in desperation around the smug small-town High Street, the bland orange lighting, the snobbishly stiff window-displays, and hit on two armless plaster models dressed in bridal gowns and veils.

I murmured, 'We lost our heads, Sergeant. You see, we've just decided to get married.'

And it worked: they went all jokey and proscriptively avuncular, and let us go. It seemed as long as you were respectable and married, or about to be, you could get away with any lewdness or crime.

It was such a good joke, such a spoof, we didn't want to let it drop.

'My fiancée here . . .' Boris would say to strangers in pubs, and their faces would compose into respect, it was hilarious to see what effect such a sober ridiculous convention could have on the most apparently wild and with-it. 'Only joking,' we'd say then, and make them confront shame-facedly their own hypocritical inconsistency, we were good at doing that to others, we never thought that one day we might have to experience it ourselves.

One Saturday evening Boris, in a tweed hunting-jacket and smoking a pipe and speaking in a cut-class accent, as he called it (a cut below the aristocracy), so fooled a company director and his wife, taking the piss out of them with tales of our Daddies' respective rural Veterinary and Medical practices, that they invited us back to supper.

Due to Boris's eloquence and eagerness to eat his worth as reparation for centuries of exploitation of the class he really represented, supper went on late and they invited us to stop over. Boris ignored my glared signals, born as much out of fear that we couldn't keep it up as a certain surprising creeping boredom, not to mention that next day we were starting exams. He said, casual as you please, Oh that was very good of them, and we repaired upstairs.

They had provided us with our first double bed. I looked at it in awe, pulling back the cover and examining the patterned non-iron sheets that were only just then appearing on the market, the kind it looked as though you ought to lie on more decorously, or have more exotic dreams between.

After he got over the shock of having to acknowledge in these bourgeoisie a lack of prudery he'd never encountered in his working-class origins, Boris took a delight in saying 'Licence without a licence!' and billowing up the sheets and pouncing out from them growling, 'Wife!', and so forth, so long into the night that we overslept next morning to find the house empty and the couple gone to work, leaving us to catch the bus back into town, and we arrived too late to make it for the first of our final exams.

We failed our BAs. But then, as Boris said, philosophy was for the birds, flapping his arms to imitate the crow-like black-winged dons. Marxism after all was subverting the traditional ways of thinking, and Aristotelian logic, which still held sway in present-day universities, had been shown to be inadequate at least a century ago.

In the end we even believed ourselves to have been liberated, we had escaped by the skin of our teeth from the trap of convention, to be free to be part of the new revolution. And anyway, said Boris, what use could a degree in philosophy be to someone who wanted a career in acting? – forgetting to wonder if it might be equally superfluous in any career of mine.

I rang my mother.

She said, 'Bronwen? Are you telling me you've failed? But that's impossible.'

I clenched my teeth. This was how much she knew me, my mother. She thought I was the po-faced swot I'd appeared to be when I first left home, that was how she wanted me to be. I felt a sudden horrible closeness of that other self: as though the air beside me shifted, as though the door of the telephone box had squeezed open, and she had squashed in beside me.

'Bronwen I don't understand.'

I said savagely, 'You don't need to understand.'

I sensed her hurt like a tangible current down the wires, and I didn't want to sense it, having to made me feel angrier still. The only way was to cut off and be cold, and even satirical:

'Oh, Bronwen, what will you do?'

I said, carrying on our current joke, 'I'm probably getting married.'

Her response completely shocked me. After all, wasn't she the one who had given up everything for it, spent half her life playing Cinderella and waiting for her prince to return? She said, 'Oh, Bronwen, you can't. Think of your future.'

So. Even in this, even if I'd wanted to get married, she would have tried to stand in my way. What kind of image of me did she have – too stuffy, too blue-stocking-dumpy even for her own pathetic narrow dream? And anyway, what insulting assumptions led her to imagine that marriage for me would be anything like her own idea of it, anything but a true partnership of equal intelligences, transcending, morally and emotionally, the social and legal strictures of a bit of paper like a marriage certificate?

After a while she said, 'Who to?'

She didn't know about Boris, I'd kept him quiet – with my mother I'd got in the habit of having a secret life.

'Another student – well, sort of.' (Boris, since on principle he never studied, and also because he liked the sound of it better, had always preferred to be called an *Undergrad*, which of course, he could now no longer claim to be.) 'He's called Boris – or rather, Archie.' Right from the beginning I found him difficult to explain.

There was a cold little silence, and then she said, seeming to lose interest, not even interested in who I

35

might be spending the rest of my life with: 'Well, you can get married in a registry office, then.'

More interested in the money than my fate.

And punishing me, I saw that, too.

Well, I wasn't going to let her.

And perhaps also, when she'd asked me the question, What will you do? a cold shudder had gone down my back. What *was* there to do at the end of the sixties for a girl who'd been led, by the Welfare State and the post-war ideal of universal education, to expect the world, but who'd been diverted and confused by sex and lack of confidence and ended up without a degree? And also, embattled with my mother, realising suddenly how estranged I'd become from my female student friends, I felt so lonely . . .

Out of fear, out of defiance, and as a joke, Boris and I got married.

We took it to extremes: the wedding was a white one.

Maggy seemed obscenely obsessed by the inconsistency.

'Look,' I said to her, as she helped me dress on the day, up in the room I used to share with my sister. 'Defiling a convention is the best way of flouting it. We can change the meaning of a symbol. We're not primitives, who believe in the power of the symbol as an entity separate from themselves. Wearing white for your wedding and being well-fucked turns a white wedding into a symbol of profanity.'

She glowered at me densely, standing there holding the veil, with her first-class pass in obsolete notions from the literature of the past, and her place in a teacher-training college, expecting to hand them on to unsuspecting future generations. Fortunately, as Boris said, children from now on would be far more influenced by the popular cultural revolution than by teachers in any institution, which he saw as the true and right socialist way, overlooking the capitalist connection – as I did too, never having got successfully into popular culture myself.

She handed me the veil with its tiara of waxed artificial flowers. It was my sister who was the bridesmaid, but, unused to conversations with me where you used the word *fuck*, and not knowing much about Boris, she'd gone off downstairs. There were tensions in the air: women who weren't your sister acting more like your sister than your real one, your real one awkward as a stranger, and your mother hovering between disapproval of the dress you'd bought with your earnings as a summer filing-clerk, and, strangely shy, wanting to show you where you might tuck it in. Strange ambivalences. A premonition, of a life without the comfort of women.

We went downstairs, where everyone was waiting, looking like the cast of an amateur production – my sister, in the vertical stripes I'd never have chosen if I'd realised how tall she'd got, my mother in her pre-war navy-blue straw, cock-eyed as a pirate's from being squashed for years at the back of her wardrobe; my Gran, and finally my thirteen-year-old-brother, with one trouser-leg caught in his sock.

'Your sock, boy,' said my Gran. 'Got the ring?' He was to give me away and double as best man. 'If you can call it that,' she added, about the ring. She didn't approve of it, it was a plaited one I'd sent off for mailorder, not wanting anything conventional; she said wedding-rings should be a pure unbroken circle to show the marriage would be likewise, and this one was twisted and full of holes.

We walked the two blocks to the church, my sister edging near the wall in case any of her old friends should see her. Someone whistled satirically and she went bright red.

The bloke who'd whistled was jumping up and down on the opposite corner; 'Cheeky bugger,' said my Gran. He wore a white linen suit and a shirt with lace down the front, and between his teeth he held a carnation. It was Boris.

'What's he wearing, his pyjamas?' asked my Gran.

I ran across, shrieking with hilarity at this arch-romance disguise, but also if the truth were known, more touched than I should have been by his turning up to our wedding looking just like Byron in white. We ran ahead arm in arm, flouting the bad-luck convention and leaving the others to follow on like the cast of Uncle Tom Cobbley.

During the service my brother made sure he got a speaking part; instead of staying silent and handing over the ring when asked if he'd got it, he said 'Yes,' in a kind of yowl, and everyone jumped. It was the first time his voice showed signs of breaking. Now my shoulders started shaking: I'd been having trouble keeping a straight face since Boris had winked at me lewdly when I'd promised to obey him.

Afterwards when my mother threw confetti, it came out

in a lump and bounced off my chest, the shop she'd brought it from must have been damp, and we'd have appeared on the photos doubled up laughing if my brother hadn't gone and put the film in all wrong.

'What a kill,' said Boris, as the train gathered speed towards our weekend honeymoon destination, pulling the marriage contract out of his pocket like a programme at the end of a play. And there were the names of the actors, and beside them their credits. I stared. *Bronwen O'Donald, Spinster.* And in the column before it, *Archibald Percival Hawfield, Bachelor.* My heart wobbled and ducked like a jelly tapped by a spoon. *Archibald* and *Percival.* What terrible names. I'd never thought of *Archie* much, but even when I had I'd never imagined it standing for *Archibald.* And *Bachelor.* Bachelors of course were men who lived with their mothers and had leather patches on their sleeves.

And where was this mother, who'd worried about currants and sewn the patches on his elbows, and from whom in recent weeks he'd been mumbling about being estranged? Did she even know about the wedding?

I sat back, and the cold plastic seat struck through my cotton honeymoon dress. I'd married a man I didn't know, whose full name I'd only just discovered, a man who'd once looked like a small-town bachelor, who probably once wore short trousers like upside-down crisp-bags, like the boys in the choir in my chapel-going phase.

The certificate trembled to the train's vibrations, the names in the boxes official and inexorable.

10

After that I didn't find it so easy to forget certain things conveniently.

I kept asking, 'So what about your mother?' and he'd give me different answers. One time he'd say, 'Basically, when I went to university I ran away.' Another: 'She disowned me.' And yet another: 'Oh, she's just crazy.' – all over his shoulder, en route to the bread-bin or the jar of peanut butter whose constant presence he so melodramatically owed to her. Till in the end he would stop, and turn to face me, and say, 'Look. What's with all this? You want to contact her, right, and set up some little note-comparing scene? You want an in-law, you want a conventional family set-up?' Which of course I didn't, and so retreated, intimidated by his slick new American-type theatre style.

He said, 'Don't hassle me, right?'

Starting out as it did, I found what we had hard to think of as marriage, but it trapped me just the same, and I lived a lonely life. I soon stopped going to Boris's opening nights. Remembering him as he had been, as I often did after the wedding, I couldn't see his acting as anything but posturing; I hated praising him insincerely, but as soon as I spoken my mind we always had a row. It seemed I'd been viewing him through rose-tinted binoculars; in reality he was smaller, and crabbier, and much further away.

He spent a lot of time away. Although in the beginning he didn't get much work, he went off a lot, doing auditions and building contacts, as he called it, the phrase my father used to use, before he left us altogether.

Once he got work, I always went with him, to avoid that awful thing of being a woman left behind. But then more often than not I'd end up sitting in our temporary flat, listening to my stomach rumble, while Boris no doubt was doing his good chap act in the theatre bar and cadging a pie.

Temporarily resident and without a degree, I found myself devoid of social contacts and serving burgers in cafes.

'Don't let anything happen,' the Biology mistress had warned us on leaving day, she meant like the girl who'd had to give up already. But you didn't have to get pregnant to end in a mess: I'd let Boris happen. I'd let him be his own happening, and as a result nothing else was going to happen for me.

We were very, very poor. While England boomed, and the department stores glittered, and exotic vegetables began to appear in the supermarkets, Boris and I lived in our threadbare jeans off bread and spuds and baked beans. In fact Boris didn't mind the diet, it was the sort of food he liked, but of course there was never enough. In spite of poverty, though, it seemed to me I was getting fat, through inactivity, no doubt, and a disordered metabolism due to depression; no wonder Boris was going off sex – come to that, so was I.

I began to feel ill. Getting up in the morning I'd feel breathless; climbing stairs would make me giddy, and going out to the shops to find what I could afford was a physical trial.

I did have moments of thinking that my life shouldn't

41

be like this, of not believing it was my necessary destiny. Mind over matter, I'd think; intelligence over material conditions. And I'd determine to find a decent job that was worthy of me, and go to the mirror and put on some makeup and tie up my hair. But my face would loom back, still white and flabby and oh-dear-what-can-the-matter-be, the face of a sluggish dependent unemployable woman, tarted up with a mad stick-on mouth. Or a witch, as three-sided mirrors showed me, my nose grown long and pointed without my knowing all those years when I'd had it stuck in books.

I thought of my childhood drawings, one fairy-tale princess after another, identical apart from details of dress or tiara, they were all meant to be smiling, but one slip of the pencil could make them look evil or silly or mad. I looked like them. I'd cut them out and stuck them down, over and over, a doodle, an obsession, with figures out of fantasy, women who'd never last in the real solid world. I'd been drawing myself.

I collapsed with grief across the dressing-table, my life seeming over at the age of twenty-four. Grounded. *I've got a part that would suit you*, he'd said, *Down to the ground*.

With time on my hands, I ought to start reading again, but then where had it ever got me? – there must be some other strategy for coping, more to do with real life, more matter and less mind, and which spending my adolescence reading had caused me to miss out on. I eyed my dusty old course-books, and felt oppressed: Boris was right, these were the books of the past, not only of the past of Western civilisation, but of a personal past of mine that had led me nowhere. There must be different books now, new ideas, I supposed, springing up out there in the swirling affluent world, but they'd be beyond me, my brain had got addled, I'd got left behind. In any case, I couldn't afford them.

I'd hand over the money for a bag of carrots or a loaf and wonder idly how many pages of a book it would buy me. One day, suddenly, it struck me to wonder how many sheets of drawing-paper it would buy.

I stood at the art counter in W. H. Smiths. The brushes gleamed, the paint-tubes glittered. I felt like an intruder at an altar for which I didn't know the rituals. I walked away, feeling foolish.

But I saved; I bought us fatty bacon instead of lean, and tins of pilchards when we could have had mince.

Guiltily, I went back and bought myself brushes and five tubes of paint.

I sat in front of the flattened cardboard box I'd laid on the table. Boris was out. The brush felt awkward in my hand. I chose red paint. I felt afraid. Perhaps I should stop, before I proved myself a failure. I had no subject. Perhaps I should go and make the supper.

I stroked the brush across the card.

Later that night, far too late for supper, and just as well, since I'd forgotten about it anyway, Boris came home.

He said, 'Yuk! What the hell is it?'

He looked around. He seemed to think it must be someone else's painting, and that perhaps they were still there. A look of suspicious jealousy crossed his face. I think that was the moment painting got tied up in my mind with the idea of infidelity, though because of the cost the guilt was already there.

I said, 'I'm not sure, it just came.'

He looked at me aghast then, as if he feared for my state of mind.

I stood beside him and surveyed it. It was a huge cross-section of a heart inside which small human figures were swinging on the valves and using them as catapults.

He said, 'What does it mean?'

I said defensively, 'I'm not sure yet, it's a work of intuition.'

He snorted, and went off to get himself his current favourite supper of dry Weetabix with butter on. After a bit he came back, and said through a cascade of crumbs:

'I should keep my intuition to myself, if I were you.'

Of course he was right. How could anything I painted have any touch with reality or the contemporary world? I'd lived cut off; we didn't buy the papers because Boris usually read them at the theatre, and nothing in recent years had prompted me to start listening to the radio, it reminded me of my Dad. If I did happen to have heard the news, well, that only gave Boris the chance to be a political bore.

I did sit up and notice, though, when they landed on the moon, jumping about like little boys on a cosmic trampoline, I stood and watched it through the window of a TV rentals shop, the image duplicated over and over, like the words on the hoardings: 'A Giant Leap for Mankind', which sure enough had been my Dad's words, more or less, when they'd first put the Sputnik up. All news was a bad recurring dream, and nothing to do with reality at all.

But Boris, and everyone else out there in that world he belonged to, knew it as reality, and they expected things like paintings to embrace it. I pushed my painting away where Boris wouldn't see it and be reminded to be scornful. I put the brushes and paints in my old leather case.

My Dad gave me that case. I nearly chucked it out once, but it's not easy with a hard-up background to throw things away.

11

I went on painting. In secret: it was a compulsion, a regression. Only this time instead of princesses it was A-level Biology cross-sections, internal human organs, livers and brains littered with beer-cans and sprouting Sputniks and harbouring snakes and nasty little Hieronymus Bosch figures doing things like snapping rubber bands.

I felt ashamed, of its automatic nature, and of the amount of time I spent on it. It was like drink or drugs, I imagined, or an extramarital lover, it filled the gaps where there'd been no decent work or friends and no husband at home. I looked less conscientiously for jobs, working only when I needed to replenish paints. I don't know what Boris thought I was doing all day with my time. Ironically, it was unnerving to discover how easy it was to keep a secret from him. He never noticed the large flat brown parcel, growing gradually thicker, which I found hard to hide when we moved. He never seemed to detect any smell, or maybe he assumed it was detergent, it seemed that Marxist ideology didn't stop him taking for granted the idea of a woman, without either the means or rewards of production, keeping a stable clean home.

This might have struck me more forcibly, and earlier than it did, if I hadn't been so lustfully preoccupied with painting, and if that hadn't given me a new sexual energy which made me as positive towards Boris when he was there to go to bed with as I was glad to be free to paint when he wasn't.

At length, though, when the paintings comprised a more or less complete catalogue of human inner components, I took stock. Four years now since we'd got married. Boris, in his poorly-paid way, was making steps forward in his career; once or twice he'd even got some well-paid hack-work, some telly bit-parts and one or two commercials – all quite against his principles of course, but financing his travel to the more meaningful auditions, a necessary evil means that would be justified by the politically-moral theatrical end. Once or twice we even had steak for supper, and a nasty red wine that he bought for its name, Bull's Blood.

But what about me? What had I got to show for those years? A pile of cardboard and paper I couldn't even ask anyone to acknowledge.

And then I began to feel resentful. So what if it was rubbish? Why should I not at least have the opportunity of having it judged? Why should I let Boris write me off so easily?

I decided, at a time when we were living in London, to try and do something with the paintings.

Not that I had the courage of my convictions, of course – not that I ever had any conviction at all. I still felt foolish about the paintings, and now, more than ever, foolish about the self and life they undoubtedly revealed. What a fool, to have hung around like that for Boris all those years. Why hadn't I just dug my heels in and refused to follow him, and made a life for myself? Why hadn't I, say, taken a course? I was aware, through my insular haze, that out there in these austerer mid-seventies there was a new, tougher breed of woman to whom my reasons – that I'd been too scared, of being even more alone than I was, of destroying the only thing I had, too scared of academic failure again, too scared of going back and admitting I'd made a mistake – all these would seem like weakness. And yes they were. I'd been a coward, a stay-at-home girl again, because home might be boring, but at least it was safer, things didn't happen.

So I didn't tell Boris what I'd decided to do. With so little confidence, I couldn't give him the chance of destroying it altogether, or despising me for having kept my painting secret in the past.

Also, something else: I strongly didn't want to share it with him.

In order to take slides I'd need to use his camera when he wasn't there. There was a hitch, though, it contained a half-used film. I embarked on my first conscious manipulation.

47

I said airily, 'Why don't you finish that film up on the dress-rehearsal tonight, and then we can see the pics you took in Edinburgh last year?'

He looked surprised, then said, 'OK,' and went on munching his Shredded Wheat with currants, insultingly uncaring about my motives, but also pathetically innocent and foiled.

I knew then exactly how secret adulterers feel.

Thus it was that making my paintings public involved me in deeper subterfuge. And because I couldn't face a public failure, leave alone have Boris hear about it, I decided I'd have to use another name. After that, my guilt lessened a little. It was as if the person involved in all this was no longer me.

Guinevere Knight. I dressed her up in the Oxfamshop clothes I'd bought for Boris's early openings: a long floral skirt, an Indian scarf and a floppy-brimmed hat. Mildly hippy she looked, and not a bit like me, except of course for that face, familiar as ever, a white maggoty blob. As Boris said, we lived in a culture sold on physical beauty, and plain blobby faces wouldn't sell paintings, nor, therefore, convince exhibitors of talent. I pulled the scarf up and the hat-brim down and stuck some large dark sun-specs over my own. I should have made the connection, they were the specs I'd bought at the seaside with Boris, another time when I got myself into more than I'd bargained for.

It was hard, I had discovered, to get anyone even to agree to look at my slides. Finally, I'd got an interview in a small avant-garde gallery. I sat, twisting my fingers nervously while the manager flipped them like a pack of cards against his lamp. Eventually, he slapped them down. He seemed to smirk. He said, 'Why don't you go to college and learn biological illustration?'

My heart dropped into my diaphragm which caught it like a trampoline and sent it bowling up again. I reached out to retrieve the slides from his cold clear view where I should never have let them get to in the first place, and knocked them on the floor. I scrabbled on all fours, my hat-brim obscuring things, my scarf slipping and tangling; I scooped them up and beat a quick retreat.

As I reached the door he said, devastatingly kind, 'I imagine you would do a nice school textbook, or one of those women's things . . .' and with a cold little shock I came up against the knowledge that, whatever the intrinsic merits or otherwise of your work, if you were a woman people approached it with cynicism as to the possibility of its having an intrinsic merit at all. I'd never know anyway; it had all been a waste of time.

I wandered along the early-evening side-streets, losing my way, struggling blindly with the A-Z, forgetting I was wearing the dark specs, and becoming progressively more uncomfortable around the crotch and hips: it was clear now why the skirt had been relegated so quickly, in the height of its fashion, to the Oxfam shop – it had the property of riding up at one side when you walked and somehow simultaneously dragging your tights down. Eventually the gusset of my tights arrived at my knees. I moved into a shop-doorway and stepped out of them.

I looked up and jumped. Through the trendy arch-shaped glass of the door, a scrawny woman in a hat was rolling a piece of cloth, and looking towards me, and then, weirdly, she divided into two, into a woman and a man. The man, a real man, had detached himself from what I realised now was my reflection, and was coming to unlock the door. I caught the name above: *The Magic Carpet*.

He put out his head and velvet-jacket shoulders. A young man, of the new male generation risen while my back was turned to exercise its right to guard the portals of the city from lone sluttish women undressing themselves.

He said, 'Come in.'

Behind him I saw the gleam of glass on paintings in an exhibition.

He agreed to show the paintings. Overnight, he made them a success.

But I never got rid of the feeling that what had attracted him was not so much my talent as the sight of me taking my tights off, my female indisposition.

12

Paintings that denounce our mechanised society with images of startling originality . . . work of strenuous intelligence and deeply committed social conscience . . .

I stared at the notice, my heart knocking as if indeed

its valves were being used as catapults. I felt triumph, vindication, regret that I'd hidden beneath an assumed identity, and yet relief that I had, and a sense of fraudulence and shame.

'Are you reading a paper?' asked Boris, incredulous and offended; such activity had come to be his exclusive right.

Perhaps now, after all, I should tell him. 'This painter here . . .' I began, but he shot me a look of such knowing contempt – might have known she wasn't actually filling the gaps in her political knowledge – that I shut my mouth and stopped, as much out of animosity and rebellion as nervousness, and went back to the article. My liver picture, with its beer-cans and miniature church-organs propped in the vesicles, was being taken as a comment on the politically sclerotic consequences of our society's growing religion of alcohol and drugged material indulgence – it seemed that some unripe raspberries in the picture had been mistaken for bunches of grapes.

That afternoon the phone rang. A male voice said, 'Hallo, love, Guinevere Knight?'

I said, 'No.' – out of truthfulness, a total lack of identification, and then I suddenly clicked and put down the phone in horror.

'For security,' Jason Fulbright, my exhibitor, had said, when he'd taken my phone-number; it didn't feel like security to me.

Later it rang again; the same voice, insolently familiar, making me think of artificial velvet. A name that sounded like Bender. 'Guinevere Knight, love?'

51

'No,' I said, and then: 'Yes,' and both sounded like lies, the latter the bigger.

Could he come and talk to me about these paintings of mine that seemed to be getting such good reviews; the readers of their arts mag would be interested, he thought, in how I worked, and where – a picture maybe of me sitting in my studio?

How could I talk to anyone about my paintings when I knew less about them than they did? 'Oh, no sorry,' I said, breaking out in a sweat, and put the phone down.

When Boris came home next day I said, 'I've had the phone number changed, and made ex-directory.'

'What?' He dropped a knife. There wasn't much that could distract him from his food. 'What the fuck if my agent's been trying to get hold of me? You know damn well I'm waiting to hear from the Walking Disasters!'

I rather knew how he felt: it had been shockingly easy, although the phone was in his name: I'd simply rung up and declared myself his wife and they'd done it on the spot.

Which shows the power of marriage. Anyone could do it to you, wipe you off the record by simply posing as your spouse.

I said miserably, 'I've been getting obscene phone calls,' and somehow it didn't seem too far from the truth.

He said callously, 'I shouldn't have thought you'd have let that worry you.'

I looked at him slapping luncheon-meat on his bread. He seemed so sure. Even I wasn't sure how I'd react to an obscene phone-call. But then I wasn't sure of anything about myself, I was beginning to get quite confused. It occurred to me to wonder how Guinevere Knight, this painter I was posing as, would react.

In the next days the listings magazine published an article by a freelance journalist called Bonder which made mention of Guinevere Knight's brisk treatment of journalists and total indifference to the opinion of the outside world.

Some days later, another weekly, accepting these facts as given, drew what they called the obvious connection with the uncompromising nature of her work, its unconventional materials and brushwork, its refusal to conform to non-figurative norms.

I began to feel quite out of it. I had an urge to look at my work myself, in the light of what was being said. Nervously, in my hat and scarf and dark glasses, I went down to The Magic Carpet.

Inside there was a man aiming little white explosions at the paintings with a camera. There was another, evidently with him, scribbling notes. Both were dressed in black with bags and equipment hanging from gunstraps. Both were chewing. Jason Fulbright, in his velvet jacket, hovered around.

Just as I was backing out, Jason bellowed, 'This is the painter!' and the rest of us jumped.

'Ah!' said the men, and the one with the notebook zoomed towards me pointing something; I flinched; there was a flash.

'Bounder,' he seemed to say. It was his hand he was holding out towards me. 'We spoke on the telephone. Miss Knight. So you do emerge now and then?'

He chewed at the side of his mouth, showing his canine tooth. He flicked his eyes back towards the paintings. 'Unique.'

For a second I thought he'd said 'Yuk.'

'Would you answer a few questions?' He sounded vaguely American, these days people I was afraid of sounded American rather than like the BBC.

'A few words about your method...' (Quick scribble) '... These works here have been so displayed as to reveal their execution on cardboard boxes, and the brand-names are clearly visible...'

Jason Fulbright had arranged the framing for me; I looked in horror over Bounder's shoulders and saw that he was right.

'... this is quite clearly a satirical attempt to break with elitist convention, but may I ask you, Miss Knight, is the choice of brand-names significant?' (Ironic grin.)

I shook my head miserably.

'Ah-hah!' (Mouth clamped shut, gum shifted to the front; scribble; nibble-nibble.)

'When do you research?'

My mouth fell open.

'Do you have a strict daily schedule?'

The questions fired, I shrugged my shoulders, I hung my head, furiously he scribbled. The camera flashed again.

'A bit about your background. Was your family artistic? Your mother? How about your father?'

'I haven't got one!' I'd said it before I knew it. I stood in shock, listening to the echo of the words in my head.

Piercing look. 'Which?'

I didn't know – either, both. My mother would have

died to know what had become of me, as well as say she'd told me so, as far as I could I kept away from her and hardly ever went home.

'A family.'

'Ah. Orphaned? Refugee, right?' (Good hard look at my nose; it was more or less the only part of my face that was visible.)

I said helplessly, 'Look . . .'

Grin; chew; significant look at the cameraman who said then, though with an equally ironic grin, 'Stick to the work, eh, Guy, give the lady a break?' At which my heart sank even further.

Knowingly: 'OK, OK.' Scribble again. Sudden intent rolling of gum between sharp incisors. Then: 'Well, there have been plenty of definitions made by others now of your work, Miss Knight, but how would you yourself define it?'

My mouth gaped.

He drew a breath; I heard it hiss.

'If pressed . . .?'

I thought: *Biological Art*, it was the best I could do, I opened my mouth to say it, but what came out was, 'Blart.'

'Eh?' Suspension of all masticulatory movement.

'I mean . . . Biological Art.'

Short silence, then: 'I see.' (Snigger.)

I turned away. I could just imagine the headline: DUMB HOUSEWIFE BLUNDERS INTO ART WORLD.

'Your phone's been out of order,' said Jason Fulbright when they'd gone.

'Oh dear,' I said, lying pointlessly, it was all up, they'd all seen through me: closer inspection revealed now that Jason had marked the worst of the paintings with black bad-mark stickers, like a teacher's disapproval or a warning against contamination; it took me moments to register that they were signs that the paintings had been sold.

Bonder's profile was published, alongside a picture of the hat with my nose protruding beneath it: ICONO-CLAST AND ICON – *A rare interview with Guinevere Knight*.

Enigmatic and aloof as Mona Lisa, Guinevere Knight yet embodies all the qualities of wit and iconoclasm for which her paintings are known. Of evident European extraction, and clearly employing the detached eye that a history of dispossession and exile can lend, she nevertheless refuses to discuss her background or personal life. Contextualisation is after all a main target of this satirical painter:

'I do not make a conscious choice when selecting brand-named cardboard boxes to paint on; to do so would be merely to create, all over again, a traditional structure of expectation. The point is to break down structures, challenge expectations.'

Attempts to trap her art in the structure of definitions, needless to say, make this imperious painter particularly scornful. Pressed to venture a definition herself, she counters roundly with 'Blart' (Biological Art), as obscenely comic a put-down as any journalist could dread.

13

Guinevere Knight's sharp dismissal of the structures of the male-dominated art establishment (not to mention her reported sharp dismissal of Bonder) had won her the respect of feminists. On a listings-mag letter-page, a feminist complained of the male assumptions in the paper's critique, particularly regarding the brain piece. This painting, in which snakes and women carrying aerosols floated along the convolutions of grey matter, had been interpreted by the male Visual Arts writer as a statement of the human conflict between on the one hand reason (which he saw as represented by the brain itself) and civilisation (the contemporary aids to cleanliness and beauty), and on the other, natural, primitive sensuality, as represented by the snakes.

But had this critic not noticed, asked the feminist correspondent with fine ironic wonder, that the people in the painting carrying the deodorant cans and pursued along the convolutions by snakes, were actually WOMEN? What was this WOMAN BLINDNESS? The artist, surely, was making a statement rather about the condition of WOMEN, not mere HUMANITY (by which we all knew men meant themselves)? The painting accurately exposed WOMEN as weighed down by the responsibility of nurture (the deodorant cans, etc.) which MEN have seen fit to relinquish themselves, our intellect (the grey matter) expended too constantly on matters of domestic toil. At the same time we were expected to be the symbols and recipients of male lust (the snakes). Cosy decent mother and temptress;

cleaner-up of shit and unsoiled virgin – all those contradictory things rolled into one.

And as for the critic's attempt to imply that the snakes represented some kind of natural innocence, well come off it, she wrote: let's acknowledge at long last that a snake is a snake is a phallus is a phallus and no amount of effort to frame Eve will work any more.

I thought that very clever, and went red with shame that none of it had occurred to me in the painting of the picture, and since it hadn't, I was inclined to believe this interpretation only marginally more than the others. I was afraid, rather, that the piece revealed things about me that people had yet to see but sooner or later undoubtedly would, and, now that it had been pointed out, the sexual connotation of the snakes embarrassed me terribly.

All the pictures but the brain piece sold. Jason was mightily pleased. Having gone into exhibition as a sideline (to what, I was never quite sure) he had earned a reputation overnight as a dealer with a nose.

'Just shows what a bit of mystery can do,' he said, crossing the gallery towards me, trendy laconic entrepreneur, and reached out and tweaked up the brim of the hat I was now in the habit of wearing, indeed, had reached a state of such shamed panic I daren't go without.

He kissed me lightly on the lips, and dropped the brim and wandered off.

It was a close shave.

Also it did unexpected things to my body.

'Can't you get your phone fixed?' he said. 'I may need to contact you in a hurry.'

'Why?' I asked; I was finding it hard to concentrate.

'Schemes,' he said mysteriously, and tapped his straight slim nose. 'Contacts.'

His room at the back of the shop was stamped with the philosophy that those who were productive were those who were pampered, the filing-cabinet and typewriter submerged in a profusion of pot-plants and Indian cushions. He spread himself out on the Indian-cloth-covered divan, and smoked the joint he'd just rolled. I sat beside him gingerly, eyeing his dangerously aesthetic slim ankles.

'The thing is,' he said, expounding his theory of how to sell culture, 'you have to know public whim.'

His hand came lightly down on my shoulder. He knocked the hat, and I had to straighten it.

'Indeed, it's a question of intuiting beforehand what the next whim will be . . .'

His hand had moved down my arm, he was stroking it lightly, almost unconsciously, with all the casual sexual familiarity that had come about in this outside world of the Pill. Beneath my hat, I went hot, with old-fashioned steamy lust.

He stood up, and I keeled over, discovering I'd been leaning on him.

'It's a question rather, I suppose, of creating the next whim, on the grounds of the present one, and knowing when the point of saturation for the present one will be.'

He was taking off his blouson shirt. His chest gleamed

with little gold hairs. Then his fashionable bags: one flick at the waist-band and they dropped to reveal expensive tiny briefs printed with butterflies.

I stood up, in horror at what was happening.

He put his hands on my shoulders; he was saying something about my own point of saturation; I said quickly, 'I'm not on the Pill.'

He said, 'Oh,' in great surprise and drew away and said, 'Oh, sorry,' as if he'd done something like bring me the wrong drink at a party.

I suddenly realised what he'd been saying: 'There'll be a point of saturation with this enigma gimmick; it's probably time you showed your face on the Box.'

He was putting on his trousers, casual and polite. I stood, with my hair and dark specs on, panicked and discomposed.

That night I had a dream in which a naked man kept walking towards me over quicksands, without sinking. He never got to me. Each time, just before he did, the dream would go back to the beginning, like a slipping film, so that he kept coming over and over again. I felt I should know him, but I couldn't work out where from.

I woke, and slept again, and had another dream in which I was doing the washing and came across a pair of underpants with green caterpillars printed all over them, and I knew they weren't Boris's, so they must be Jason's, and just then I heard Boris coming up the stairs so I shoved them in a cupboard, incriminating evidence, dripping wet as they were. Boris entered and said, 'I'm going fishing, where's my bait?' and I knew straight away they weren't underpants at all, they were his fisherman's muslin bag and the caterpillars were real and were even now crawling out under the cupboard door. . . .

When I woke again Boris was sitting on the bed slurping up his breakfast, with strands of Shredded Wheat dangling out of his mouth. He turned and said, 'Oh, hello, do you want sex?' and I said, 'Yes, if you wipe your mouth first.'

Afterwards, I did this really dreadful thing, I called him 'Jason' by mistake, but luckily he didn't hear.

Jason showed me an article in an alternative listings mag.

. . . One is prompted to wonder how far dealers will go in deception, and it has been suggested that on occasion what has been presented as individual talent has in fact been the work of deeply cynical commercial syndicates. One current case which falls under suspicion is the successful Guinevere Knight exhibition at The Magic Carpet gallery run by Jason Fulbright, whose shady dealings have more than once been exposed by this magazine. Guinevere Knight is a shadowy figure, never appearing in public and unobtainable by telephone; it is quite possible that she doesn't exist. True to his well-recorded impertinent character, Mr Fulbright uses this convenient enigma as his very selling gimmick. What makes his activities particularly pernicious is that The Magic Carpet receives sizeable Arts Association funding. Is The Magic Carpet taking the tax-paying public for a ride?

He said, 'These disaffected lefty graduates, they've got to have a whipping-post.'

He handed me a cheque. There seemed an awful lot of noughts. An awful lot of money for my guilty random impulses. The cheque was made out to Guinevere Knight, not me.

He said, laughing cynically now over the article, 'Saturation point, I told you. We'll give them an invite to the press reception.'

'What press reception?' I said in a panic. 'But we've sold all the paintings!'

'Except the brain piece,' he reminded me.

'No,' he said briskly, 'this is the night you give 'em a face to keep 'em going till next time.'

As I'd known all along, in the end, you can't sell a thing without a face and a body. And: next time. There wasn't going to be a next time, I knew that now. I'd done no painting at all since I'd finished all the organs, as if, disgorging them all, those bits of body, I'd left myself empty, an anonymous shroud with no substance beyond that which others cared to impose, doing what they liked with it.

But as he said, there came a saturation point. How could feminists, with their codes of solidarity and democracy, go on in their allegiance to someone now awarded the title 'gypsy princess', if she didn't rise up and publicly disown it and prove it unworthy?

And the other, opposing faction, the one with all the power? The brain piece was a sign of the way they would turn – the bit of body left behind, unacknowledged, stamped with the dirty word feminism.

There was no future in any of it, no next time to promise at any press reception. When Jason's reception took place I wouldn't be there.

I said to Jason Fulbright, 'I'll be there.'

'Great,' he said, 'I knew you would.'

(He knew she would. Guinevere Knight. The woman he imagined there beneath the hat. She was a woman who knew her own mind. She must have a purpose. She did. She and I were growing closer in this hour of need.)

I said: 'That is, if you'll do something for me.'

Grin. 'There's a catch?'

'Oh, it's just a little thing.' I leaned against one of his jungle-strewn tables, easily, languidly, trying out Guinevere Knight's bones. 'I've got this friend,' I said. 'She's been in South Africa with her husband, but now the marriage has broken up, and she's come back on her own and she needs to find work. What she'd really like to do is illustrate, but because of the marriage, she never got round to training or getting any experience, and she really needs some kind of break.'

I smoothed Guinevere Knight's hand along Guinevere Knight's thighs. It was heady, almost sexual, this feeling of possessing her, I could have almost gone through with the reception.

I said, 'With all your contacts, do you think you could manage something?'

'Yeah, sure,' he said.

I smiled confidently, possessing Guinevere Knight completely, it seemed, before I killed her altogether.

'What's her name?'

63

I'd thought about this carefully. I was going to be myself again, but I didn't want to be too traceable.

'Bronwen O'Donald.'

He said callously, cruelly, 'What is she, some kind of hybrid Celt?'

And it sounded odd to me too, though not in the sense of being eccentric or unusual, but as if I were speaking of a semi-stranger, someone I'd known only vaguely, and a long time ago.

I thought that meant I'd overcome things.

'I had a word with my chum in publishing,' said Jason. 'Here's the number your poor little friend should ring.'

The note of charity stabbed me, and the mistake I made in years after was to forget how conditional my escape had been on the cynical charity of the network of men.

'Thanks,' I said, and he kissed me, knocking my glasses crooked and put his hand briefly on my breast before he remembered: 'Oh, yes, sorry, no Pill.'

I slipped the number in my pocket, and looked around the gallery walls. There they were, all the bits of my life to date, the church organs that boys in crisp-bag trousers could sing to, rubber bands that boys could snap, and beer-cans and aerosols and Sputniks for littering up the universe – all the images that, because of their place in my past, could make my heart flap, my liver vibrate, my grey matter crawl. The inside story. Random images, yet horribly connected, each new event in my life carrying a legacy, as if I'd never been able to leave the past behind.

Well, now I would. I'd disgorged it all.

Jason was waiting, in the arch of the doorway through which I'd first seen him. I walked past. I would not let myself vibrate because men walked through archways. I left him, and the paintings, behind.

On the evening of the reception, I couldn't resist going past in my brown gaberdine mac and a headscarf. I stopped at a window opposite and watched the guests dribbling in. I didn't wait to see them start to come out again, amused or triumphant at the painter's non-appearance.

The wind was getting up, it was autumn, and the nights were drawing in. I felt sad. I felt like a murderess, who after the act must relinquish the glory.

There was some speculation afterwards of scandal, and one hint of murder (at which I started quite guiltily).

For a while I had the feeling of being followed. One afternoon I came out of the flat to go shopping and thought I saw a man dart backwards in the foyer below.

When Guinevere Knight didn't reappear, though, and no more of her paintings came to light, interest died, renewing briefly, just once: They thought they'd got the body as Jason always said they must: A woman was dragged naked from the Thames.

One day I came across a book of Boris's which at the time of my foray into the art world he'd been using for a collective dramatisation for Theatre in Education on the subject of feudal ethics. *Guinevere and the Naughty Knights*.

I'd really thought I'd made it up.

Five years later no one had heard of Guinevere Knight.

I had my illustration. It was safer. My own ideas had proved too dubious and uncontrollable; I felt a whole lot safer illustrating and interpreting those of others.

Almost straight away I went back to using the name Hawfield. It was better that way, no one would trace me. Bronwen O'Donald once more ceased to exist. And I discovered that now I felt almost comfortable with Boris's name. I was beginning to feel almost comfortable with Boris altogether; it made a world of difference to our relationship for me to have an income to myself and the relative dignity of my own work, I found. We'd come to terms; we'd got quite matey; we stopped having sex again, and this time round I didn't mind. Life was simpler without it, and I didn't feel as if I'd ever be interested again.

14

Morning. The skylight in my attic is a pale patch like the place where sticking-plaster's been ripped off skin.

I open the door to the stairs. Silence. I look over the bannister: a deep soft rabbit-hole where Alice could fall.

As I stand there, the phone rings in the darkness below. I draw back. The sound rises like bubbles, like gas. It can't be for me, of course, no one knows I'm here – or do they? It goes on bubbling, a poisonous wish from a well. Then on the ground floor a door opens, and the ringing stops abruptly; a male voice answers and a brief conversation follows, muffled, I can't hear the words. I wait, a ghost, a Listener without substance, clinging to the solid wall. Then the clatter and ping as the phone is put down again, and the door shuts on silence once more.

I go on down to the bathroom.

I pull my sleeves up at the sink, and stare at my arms. Overnight a rash has developed among the bruises: red lumps running together in ugly weals. Like whip-marks, like disintegration burns at the radioactive end of the world.

When I open the door there's someone on the stairs, above and coming down. I push it to again. A woman passes, through the crack I see pale wispy hair and the floating fabric of a dress; she goes on down, not stopping at the kitchen, not stopping to eat: an actor, trained to do anything, even live off air.

The house coming to life, opening its eyes and ears. And then it strikes me what the rash is: the house coming to life, but not just human, there must be livestock in that bulging stained mattress, or in the floorboards, between the cracks of dingy plaster, stirring, uncurling, coming to life at the smell of me, my all too human substance, after all.

I reached the top. My door is open, which is not how I left it. As I step towards it, something pounces, a roar: the sound of a Hoover. My room is being cleaned.

The pinafored figure bends and stretches, straightens briefly to nod and then bends again, pushing the dragon-head, spreading hairs across the nylon, mine or

someone else's that have fallen; digging under the bed.
　Which is when the case shoots out and springs open.
　The Hoover stops.
　There rises the ghost-smell of turps.
　'Christ, what you got in there, a man?'

Nothing stays buried, *says Bron.*
　She is serious, quiet, as she gives me the next part.
　What follows is the near-side, the flip-side, of her
　story.

PART II

15

'*Nothing stays buried*' (she says). *Like splinters beneath the skin, like the egg-cells in an ovary, things move towards the surface.*

Feelings you hoped you'd never have again. That caught-out feeling: fish-hook in the guts.

Dave said, at the literary party, 'You're left-handed.'

After all, even my illustrations giving me away.

I put down my glass.

He said, 'I'm going too. I'll come with you.'

I'd lost confidence. I felt trapped.

I said, 'OK', and heard myself sound sullen.

He smirked.

However, outside, away from the smugness and smoke of the literary party, I felt less threatened. The sun was warm on the Chelsea terraces and light flickered off the leaves in the square. I was on the move, making for my train and my flat in the outer suburbs; soon I'd be at the corner where my way would branch off.

He said, 'I used to live round here.'

He had said it significantly, he'd been giving me a cue, expecting me to give him in turn the signal to expand; he wanted to be the hero of a story.

'Up there,' he said, pointing to a window slashed with orange sun. He stopped, summoning up, I could see, a seminal scene (as he'd no doubt call it) from his Great

71

Story, which naturally he'd assume to be greater than mine.

I laughed.

He turned round, his safari-jacket flapping, his ridiculous dress of Third-World-visiting male Royals, and, almost sharply, with an expression I interpreted as lecherous curiosity, said, 'Are you married?'

I nodded, and he said nothing.

And then we reached the King's Road, where our ways were different, and he turned to me briefly with a look of sudden irony, and said, 'So am I.' He was laughing at me, and then he was off across the road, darting between the cars and putting the flow between us: he seemed to leap, one hand on a bonnet, his large frame pivoting on one surprisingly slim wrist, making the driver hoot and swear, and then landed high and dry on the other side.

And the traffic got going, a flashing stream beginning to hurtle, and he stood grinning and tapping a cigarette on a packet, and the city rang with the rising notes of accelerating engines, and pigeons wheeled at the commotion, opening out the sky, and I had fallen in love.

16

Down below a cat prowled along a wall. I watched through the window, the phone at my ear. Dave's voice: 'Will you meet me?'

The cat flicked its tail. Cat, familiar. Changer of shape. You fall in love, you change shape.

The cat stopped. Feet perfectly balanced, placed each side of the slippy peaked tiles. Acrobat, balancer. Poised on the border.

It was a question of borders.

I said, 'Will you meet me?'

The cat leapt, out in the air.

He said over the phone, 'Nothing can stop us now. Not three hundred miles, or two spouses – or' (keeping it light) 'should that be spice?'

He said, casual, off-hand, but with a note of politeness that touched and amused me, 'Oh, by the way, are you on the Pill?'

Also, with a stab of anxiety he couldn't quite hide: 'I hope we recognise each other,' and then he quickly did a send-up of a romantic assignation: 'You'll know me by the chocolates I shall bring.'

Which was when I said, 'I'll send you an identikit.'

Or maybe I asked him to send one to me.

He had some business beforehand and I went on the District Line to meet him. It was sunny, early evening; pigeons made circles of restless excitement. I was a little bit late. I had stepped off the train and felt suddenly afraid. Would the thing I was about to do change my life frighteningly, for ever, open it up to an uncertain end? I went and sat in a cafe. If I didn't turn up, he'd understand. I thought of him, taunting me over the traffic: we were in the same boat, we were both in

73

a position where we wouldn't want to do anything destructive.

In which case, I told myself, it was all right to go on. I stood up and walked to meet him.

He was nervous. he thrust the chocolates apologetically towards me, he didn't carry off the joke.

He said, almost shyly, 'We ought to have wine.'

He was looking about, down the street, but ineffectively, as though he couldn't concentrate.

I felt suddenly full of confidence. Beside this nervous man, so much older and presumably so much more experienced, I who'd so often quailed and trembled now felt strong – almost calm.

I said, 'Here's a wine-shop, right beside us.'

He hesitated and turned; he seemed confused. Grey wisps of hair brushed his collar above his smooth wide back.

'No . . . this other . . .' And he began to walk a little way on.

I was touched, by his desire to please, to find the best. I was perhaps a little disappointed in his loss of wicked carelessness, missing that sense I had expected of being wicked and carefree together. But also I was amused.

'What wine do you like?' he asked.

'Oh, white,' I said, not caring, satirical, trying to encourage him.

He did smile then, and then again his brow furrowed, as he chose something special.

The hotel was a cliché. Purple carpet and bedspread, dirty lace curtains pinched in the middle.

I said, 'My God, a seedy dive. If it was a film-set they'd call it overdone.'

He came and sat on the bed where I'd collapsed in hilarious disbelief. He smiled in a way that seemed apologetic. He didn't need to, it was a question after all of flouting the clichés and rising above them. I laughed and stretched, relishing the irony of exercising twentieth-century sexual choice among the trappings of traditional sexual slavery.

He hadn't moved. He'd turned away.

I began to realise something was wrong. I sat up and leaned across.

'Whatever is it?'

He didn't speak.

And then I knew: he was trapped in the old male requirement to perform. He was far more trapped than I.

I felt sorry for him suddenly. I put my hand on his arm and said, 'It doesn't matter.'

He turned, a look of hope, or relief, coming into his face.

'Why don't we just lie down together,' I said. And we did, taking off our clothes.

His body was white, sheeny and hairless, with here and there the faint silver band of a scar, and huge pale thighs with pleated muscles. His abdomen was slightly thickened, a fact about which he was clearly shy. His physical shyness took me quite by surprise.

And also surprising, and also touching, was that he seemed to feel no right whatever to my body. He reached towards me cautiously, and ran his hands across my belly, avoiding my breasts. His penis hung

75

limp, and in spite of what I'd said, I was filled with disappointed lust.

He said, reading my mind, 'There is a reason . . .'

He avoided my eye. I waited.

'I can't use Durex.'

I had a flash of disbelief – a man like him, all the women he'd no doubt had, all those years before the Pill; I even had a second of wanting to laugh, followed by a stab of disappointment in such prudery.

But then again I saw he was troubled, and I said hastily, 'It doesn't matter,' and that was when his penis stiffened, desire at last overcoming his shyness, I thought, and he either mistook my meaning, or it happened out of lust before either of us knew it, but his penis slipped inside me and it took a lot of will-power to ask him to draw it out again.

It was curious, though, just how anxious he'd been: in those first moments, his face had been gleaming with sweat.

Later he whispered into the back of my neck: 'Do you know what really turns me on?' and I knew more or less what it was he was going to say, because we'd overcome all our problems apart from the technical one, all our awkwardness and caution, we'd become wicked and satirical again.

He whispered: 'A black lacy garter.'

And I laughed.

Perhaps I simply no longer cared: what he did, what he stood for; I'd fallen in love, I'd changed my shape, I'd opened out, I was receptive and wide as I hadn't been before. Wide as a barn door, as my mother might have said.

Another thing that bowled me over: the touching vulnerability of intimacy between strangers. Or perhaps it was simply that I didn't get an orgasm; it's hard to be cynical and dismissive when you're left with the need to be fulfilled.

17

Boris was eating sausages.

I had decided to tell him. This time, I thought, there would be no hiding, no lies. Caught myself thinking. *This time.* After all this time, my paintings still felt like unconfessed adultery – more so: as time went by and the years of silence on the subject mounted up, the degree of deceit increased accordingly, and I felt guiltier about that than I did about what was happening now. I was more sure of my right to sexual freedom than to creative talent, and more sure of Boris's acknowledgment in this.

In fact, I misjudged him. He dropped his fork. Grease splattered across the blue formica surface.

'You what?'

I didn't want to repeat it. There were no suitable words. *Affair* was so sordid. I'd said, 'I'm having a relationship with somebody else,' and that had sounded prim, evasive and defensive.

He said, incredulous, disgusted 'You mean you're having it off with somebody else?'

I cringed. I steeled myself. I said, 'And I'm going on the Pill.'

He flung his knife down, the whole plate skidded and fell off the edge of the table, he jumped up and swirled about, he put his hand on his head; I went cold; I thought, He's melodramatic; and then I wanted to laugh, until he swung back round and pain glared from his wide blue eyes, and then I wanted to cry: I was breaking up into several disparate emotions, I didn't know which was the true one, and I couldn't cope until I crystallised into coldness again.

He bent away over the kitchen surface as if nursing a pain. I thought, He can't behave like this, not after all he's always said about non-proprietorial relationships, about love being the gift of freedom and choice, about the bourgeois nature of jealousy, and most especially after the disappearance of sex from our relationship in the last few years.

He swirled round. 'Oh, Bron! Oh, God! Is it me? Is that it? Oh, I know, I'm sorry, I've been tied up in my work and all that bloody corny crap!'

'No . . .' I didn't like him putting it like that – neglected wife seeks fulfilment elsewhere – pushing that role on me: victim; denying my free will; and I noticed fleetingly also it was the possible indictment of cliché on his own part that was distressing him as much as anything.

He said, 'Listen – ' and suddenly his arms were round me fiercely, 'I can make it up, Bron, oh God, I want to – ' and then he was kissing me, gobbling, like someone starved, and I was amazed to find myself excited, and we fell together on the lino, and he slipped some Durex from his pocket, as though he'd had it there, all those years, just in case – another time I should have put two and two together – and we made passionate love right there on the kitchen floor.

Afterwards, his hair was greasy, he had got it in the plate.

And then he started asking questions, but all about Dave. Who was he, where did he live, what did he do? Hot insistent demands, that banged it all into a pigeon-hole he could condemn.

He said, 'Huh! A seedy old hack!'

He said, 'Huh! A sexist old lecher!'

'Boris, please.'

He glared, challenging.

I finished lamely, 'Don't be superficial.'

He leaned across the table, fixing me with the glare. 'OK, then, what size is his cock?'

So this was how it was with Boris when it came to the crunch.

'Well?'

I said drearily, 'Thicker than yours and shorter, if you really must know.'

He fell back. 'God, you're disgusting!'

'Why? You think your bloody prick defies comparison? Oh, I can have it poke about inside me, but I mustn't dare to speak of it, or admit that there are others beside it in the world?'

But already, as I spoke, I felt I wasn't being fair, and that in fact he'd been challenging me precisely to refuse to reduce his meaning to a piece of anatomy measurable

79

in size and interchangeable with someone else's, to prove that he meant more than just that. I'd called his bluff, and hurt him.

But then again, it was he who'd asked the question, who'd invested his importance and meaning in the size of his prick, and who'd thought of comparisons. I thought then of how he'd swept me off my feet the minute he'd known, not out of grief or love, it seemed to me now, but out of sheer possessive rivalry; as if knowledge of another man had been an aphrodisiac, and his true relationship in those moments of sex had been with the other man, and not with me. I felt sick.

'A sexist git!' he spat again, and I thought drearily that he didn't have a lot of right to judge.

But I didn't know what to think, or how to view him. He could be anything: tweedy bachelor, lefty artist, any of his numerous disguises; what was real and what was not? Nothing seemed clear, and anyone could be anything, and I didn't know how to view myself any more.

He said, banging home the stereotypes: 'I'm amazed at you, you know, falling for that.'

He said, 'You're going against all you've ever stood for. You're not acting like yourself.'

But I didn't know who she was, myself, and I knew even less as I began watching her from the side.

18

She was acting a part. There was another actor with her: an older man. Young woman, older man: a traditional alignment, which they had embraced, she believed, in order consciously to test themselves against it. Oh, Boris was right: it was an old, old, story, a well-worn one; but they weren't afraid of old stories as he was, they were fearless enough to play a game with it; they'd rewrite it altogether in the end. So she thought.

They chose a hotel that was seedy – deliberately, specifically for the feel of not belonging to that world, of being free to look around and laugh and feel superior, and over three months they went there three times, for a few short hours, dipping into the story from out of their separate lives.

'My God,' she said, 'It's a cat-house, a seedy dive, let's get out of here.'

But having said it, and laughed, she was safe in staying.

'My God,' she said, the third time, same hotel, different room, 'all the rooms are the same. There must be storage depots all over the country full of purple bedspreads and lace curtains. Seedy Dives – Direct Suppliers.'

'Fast Service,' he added, smirking, and pinned her down on the bed.

And the room in which they met was a world they could control. Tentative and careful, they didn't ask too many questions, keeping the outside world at bay, keeping both worlds separate and therefore intact. Or so she thought.

Though in fact, the world of the room infused her daily life, melting its borders, changing its shape. 'Still having it off with your filthy old feller?' Boris would ask angrily, coming upon her dreaming, the ink drying on her brush.

And when she stepped from the room the third time, forgetting that in fact it was a different one, with a different position along the corridor, she almost tumbled, like Alice in Wonderland, down the stairs.

'My God!' she said, 'Don't they clean? Just look at all the grime!'

'No time,' he said, 'Quick turnover,' and pushed her onto her belly and rolled on from behind.

They had sex half-off the bed, and on the floor, and up against the grimy sink, face to face, or stretched away, with her above, with him behind, letting go, leaping out to the borders of experience, but all the time with a kind of calculation, and – the woman thought – control.

And the woman wore a black garter, snatching it from him, and saying, 'Where does it go?' and dissolving into giggles, pushing it up her arm, then hooking it around her ear, and finally letting him slip it up her leg. And then she'd lock him round with her strong thighs, one ringed with the slave-band that she'd chosen to wear because she could also choose not to, holding him tight in a sensual contract of shared freedom and power.

Or so the woman saw it. Or told herself she saw it.

Though when she walked into the street with him, having forgotten to take the garter off, and it fell round her ankle in front of several passers-by, and she dissolved in helpless giggles, he didn't find it funny at all.

'The Real Thing,' he called it, their relationship. Like real coffee, or mayonnaise.

Or as if he meant business.

Which disturbed her.

19

It was the third time.

She ran her fingers along his faint silvery scars.

She'd asked, the first time, 'Where on earth did you get them?' and he'd shrugged, 'Here and there. Of course, the war.'

Now she wondered. She wanted to know. She wanted after all to know all about him.

He was saying, breathing wickedly on the back of her neck: 'Do you know what, besides black garters, turns me on?'

She shook her head; it made his teeth grate on her neck.

'Black stockings.'

She took out the bare facts he had given her and which she'd shoved away like idly-gathered seaside stones. He was a writer; he lived in Yorkshire, in the country. he had a wife, who'd been a teacher, but who didn't seem to work now. He had one teenage daughter. There were other facts, less complete but more vivid, like bits of broken shells among the stones: he'd been to Cambridge, he'd worked on films and TV; he'd had a lot of London media friends, though he didn't seem to see many of them now. And then that sharp piece of coral: he'd been in the war.

She started dwelling on the facts, breathing on the stones and polishing them.

But she found it hard to ask the question she wanted to. A childhood of learning not to ask followed by a twelve-year schooling with Boris in the right to personal privacy had left her practically incapable of forming the words.

Finally she blurted it:

'Does your wife know?'

He shook his head with such a slight movement that it seemed like a sign, a warning not to tread any further. And she felt ashamed, respecting as she did the privacy of his relationship with his wife, indeed, his wife's relationship with him, and expecting as she did that he would likewise respect her own life beyond these hotel walls.

But he said, 'You know . . .' and paused and tugged gently at the purple candlewick tufts, 'I want to tell you everything.'

And then he sighed, as though the telling were impossible.

He said, 'I'd like to write it down.'

20

He wrote her a letter. A sharp white envelope flicking like a tongue through the letterbox, breaking through the private seal of her life with Boris.

Boris picked it up and flapped it in her face.

'From your dirty old feller,' he said, sarcastic and angry.

She opened it, and a musty warm scent of tobacco was released.

My Darling, Dearest, Wonderful Bron.

She cringed. It was inappropriate. It read like a pressure, when of course the contract between them, she thought, was that they demanded nothing of each other – no requirement to be wonderful, or darling or dear and not each other's anything, just their vulnerable, dangerous, exploring selves.

In the letter he called her *My little Bron*. A mistake. Wrong word, *little*, in an experience she considered an expansion.

> After you'd gone on the train I went back to the hotel and cleared up your mess, you greedy girl. Chocolate papers everywhere . . .

Making her sound like a careless carefree schoolgirl.

She felt confused. Did he really see her that way? She, who had always been so painfully self-conscious, even now in her bravery tortuously self-questioning?

But then again she experienced that sense of not

knowing who she was or ever had been, and of being at a point where she could change into anything . . .

But hadn't he eaten the chocolates too — come to think of it, hadn't he eaten most of them?

. . . I kept the chocolate papers. I couldn't bring myself to throw them away . . .

She went still. Those chocolates, which surely, he'd brought each time to be satirical, and which she'd eaten partly out of sheer unsentimental hunger and partly just to join in the joke . . .

. . . I was so sad to see you go, so desolate to come back to the room alone. When I saw the papers curled where you'd laughingly thrown them, I picked them up and kept them to remind me, to keep those moments alive . . .

She had a sensation of something touching her, closing about her . . .

Had she got it all wrong, what they expected of each other, and the terms on which they were there? Had he?

Afraid, she picked up the letter again and read on. He described his day: An early rise in an old stone farmhouse amongst the Yorkshire Dales, a tiled kitchen with a coal-fired stove that must be stoked for the day; a dog that had slept beside it all night, three cats that swirled to be fed. Five hours' work on an article, at a window that overlooked his garden, and beyond that the valley. He discussed the content of the article, his ideas, his mode of approach, the politics of having it commissioned by a certain magazine.

There were glaring gaps. Not a single mention of his wife. And in her unease, looking for comfort, she told herself that that was good, that it meant that he had a proper sense of borders not to be broken; yet in her unease she needed more than ever to know.

Lunch at one (in the kitchen, or where? – he didn't say; eaten alone? Prepared by whom?) and then another two hours' work. After that a rest, which he spent writing this, and drinking coffee, freshly ground and very strong.

One of my weaknesses, strong coffee. Brandy is another, and also Turkish Delight. Also Bron.

A list of things to be consumed, irresistible, but with the power to do him harm. Was that how he saw her?

He ended: *I kept the paper from the aspirin that you took for your headache . . .*

It was true, she'd had a headache, the strain of it all had broken the fantasy in the end . . .

. . . and also the styrofoam cup that you bit in your agitation.

She went cold. She couldn't view it as he intended: herself, her memory, giving the object life and meaning; she saw it the other way round, all she could feel was that he'd reduced her to an object, a polystyrene cup with a piece bitten out of it.

I keep them on my windowsill, and glance at them as I work.

He wrote: *They are my mementoes of you.*

She had to read it again. What she'd read was: *memorials.*

Later he rang her and said he'd planted a rose for her.

She was infused with a sense of loss and dread. And knew she'd picked it up from him: He was a man deeply afraid.

But of what?

Of growing old, perhaps . . .

Or something deeper, more pervasive . . .

He took a plastic cup. He invested it with powers.

Giving in to symbols and omens. Relinquishing power to the material world. Fear of life, as much as fear of death.

She ran her gaze across the letter with its crude archaic modes of language. He was caught in a trap, a language and culture based on a debilitating dependence on the power of symbols.

She wanted to release him; she wanted to teach him to understand differently.

Or perhaps, like Boris, she simply couldn't bear to think that she'd fallen into a cliché.

21

They met again, the fourth time only, but already it was autumn and leaves in the London parks were turning brown. They would stay together two nights, they wouldn't need to be rushed and intense before she ran for a train; they could listen and talk.

He said, 'There's a lot you don't know . . .' and then stopped, as if afraid that if she did know, she'd turn away.

She felt impatient with his fear. She was brave now, she felt that the truth couldn't hurt you if you didn't let it.

She said, 'Shoot.'

He said, 'Well, I've been what you'd call a womaniser . . .'

She laughed out loud. 'I wouldn't call it that. I wouldn't call it anything. I wouldn't tuck you away in a simple-minded stereotype.'

He looked at her, searching, his large features soft with thoughtful surprise, as though she really had introduced a new concept.

She said, 'Stereotypes will overcome you if you let them. Things are always more complicated than they seem.'

'But if you knew . . .'

'Look. Whatever happened in the past doesn't have to make a difference to how things are, between us, now.'

He stared, and after a moment bent and kissed her, softly, slowly, in a way he hadn't before, and the sex this time was more truthfully close to the phrase that he always used for it, making love.

But, as in the other times with him, she didn't have an orgasm, she remained unfulfilled.

To encourage him, she talked about herself. She told him about her childhood, she spoke about Boris. She found, embarking on a hilarious description of Boris's disguises, that after all talking about Boris with Dave made her feel safe; it was as though, by doing so, rather than threatening its security, they made open acknowledgment of her primary commitment, and so ensured its safety.

'What a nutter,' he said, seeming to share her amused indulgent affection for Boris, and then kissed her lazily and fell asleep.

But later the bell downstairs woke her, people coming and going through the night. Street-light entered and showed up the room: peeling paint, cracks in the plaster forking towards the ceiling, the cornicing sliced by a partition where the next room began. Rooms divided and botched, to fit as many fleeting couplings as possible at once. Rooms drifting with the dust of impermanent liaisons, detritus there was no time to sweep up, scum in the sink, flakes of skin and limp Durex beneath the bed. An atmosphere thick with old structures and alignments. She felt breathless.

The bell went again below, a short sharp shock, a flat buzz, like the sound of those loops on wires at funfairs, when you falter . . .

Dave woke. He said, 'Business is sharp.' He seemed amused. He smoked a fag. The smoke rose, curling up the partition which looked as if it were only made of hardboard, a fire hazard, no doubt. He put his butt out, dropping ash off the table, adding to the hotel sea of dust.

He slid his hand under the pillow.

She stared, confused by what he'd drawn from under it.

Gently serious as they'd been, they weren't, surely, playing games now?

He let it fall, a sheer black stocking.

He caught her eye. He looked back at her, dead level, and then wavered, defying, pleading with her to know that after all this was no game.

He said, drawing it up her thigh, 'Do you know what else turns me on?'

And even while he asked it, her guts turned molten.

He whispered, 'Black suspenders.'

As he slipped himself inside her, the doorbell went again.

And she thought of how dogs could be trained to salivate at the sound of a bell.

He said, 'I don't know where to begin,' running his fingers on the ticklish skin inside her wrist.

They were sitting at mid-day in a restaurant window. The air outside was very still. Across the square, the odd leaf detached itself occasionally and fluttered down.

He stopped speaking, but went on stroking; as though the words had caught in his throat, words, clumsy words, being no good for what he had to say. She put her hand on his, to indicate that the attempt to tell, however messy and inadequate, would be safe.

He said, 'I once had a lot of friends . . .'

He paused.

'As a matter of fact, I've arranged for us to meet one of them today.'

91

She loosened her hold, taken aback. It was the last thing she might have expected, believing as she did that their liaison was insulated from the rest of the world.

He drew back, knocking her hand as he moved away: 'Ah, there he is! Bang on time!'

She turned, confused. A tall man in white-rimmed glasses was weaving between the tables towards them.

Dave called, 'Clive!' and beckoned him to sit down, though on arriving at the table the newcomer stood back in an attitude of survey. He was looking at her.

Then he clicked, like an actor snapping out of a part, and said, 'She's beautiful. Stamped approved.'

She was speechless. Dave was smiling, seeming well pleased. He had brought his friend in to assess her, it seemed; discussed her, evidently, beforehand – while mentioning nothing of the friend to her – and then brought him in to deliver his judgment.

But when the friend nipped away to let the waiter know he had come, Dave leaned over, shyly excited, and said, nodding backwards in Clive's direction, 'What do you think?', just as eager after all to have her judge him. And after all, she thought, seeing herself as perhaps over-touchy, hadn't there been a note of irony, of self-parody, in that outrageous 'stamped approved'?

She said, hoping not to sound grudging, 'He seems OK,' and again Dave smiled, as he had about Clive's pronouncement on her, scooping up the crumbs of approval she offered, and her heart was wrenched to see him so vulnerable, so dependent on his friends liking each other, a situation it was so hard to guarantee.

He said, 'Clive's my oldest, my best friend.' And she knew then he meant just about the only close one.

Clive stayed with them all afternoon. When they'd finished the meal, they went to a gallery, and then when the pubs were open again, for a drink. And all the time the two men discussed Clive's work on a computerised arts catalogue, and all their mutual friends – whose latest doings had to be relayed, she noticed, by Clive to Dave and never the other way round – and all their latest shows, or books, or films. And she remained outside of it all, outside their long-term understanding, a spare woman hanging on Dave's arm, a female token, a bit of occasional decoration (she began to think as the day wore on), that made the men feel better and more confident and free in their relationship with each other, the real one.

In the pub, Dave went to the loo and she and Clive were left alone. He seemed awkward and cold. She thought: Self-parody was right; he really doesn't like me.

He said, 'I've known Dave a long time . . .'

She laughed, affecting jollity, for the sake of peace, for the sake of harmony. 'I gathered that!'

It didn't work. He seemed displeased, and he lapsed into silence, and she knew then he'd meant something more, there was a special piece of knowledge he was doubting she was worthy of.

He hesitated. Then he said, 'I've always stood by him, in all his bad times . . .' and stopped.

She was being given a warning. It was clear he felt that Dave needed protection from her.

And she wanted to ask what bad times, but she was angry, at the insult, at the assumption, and at the knowing intrusion on the privacy of Dave's relationship

93

with her. She didn't want it from him, anything she found out she would find out from Dave himself. She gulped her drink in silence, angrily.

And then Dave returned, and said to Clive, 'Oh, by the way, how is Johnny?'

Clive paused. 'I forgot to tell you. He's in hospital.'

There was a current of alarm, as though this moment was one they had been dreading for years.

'It's lung cancer. He's dying.'

Ash dropped from Dave's fag and caught in his cuff.

Clive left. Dave seemed low when he'd gone, and ill at ease. The news of the dying friend had cast a shadow that her company couldn't relieve. They sat in silence.

She fingered her empty scummed beer-glass. It occcurred to her that Clive, as well as knowing, had been manipulative and cunning: not once had he mentioned Dave's wife. Or was it simply that he'd been sensitive enough to wait for a mention, and hearing none had understood that the subject was taboo? She didn't know, she couldn't tell, but in any case she didn't want any taboos.

She wanted to break down the barriers and get close. She put her arm through Dave's and squeezed it, and he turned to her slowly, and seemed to focus from a long way off, coming back slowly, and slowly, he smiled.

And that night their lovemaking was gentler than ever: as though their difficulties uncovered nerves that made them move with tender caution and tingle at the slightest touch. As if lust and passion had been softened with the brush of affection.

So she felt.

She said, petitioning his caution, 'You know, it was difficult when you wrote. It really upset Boris.'

He looked at her softly. 'I thought he didn't believe in sexual possessiveness,' and she dropped her eyes.

He curled a strand of her hair around his finger. He said, 'My wife . . .'

He released his finger. 'She's ill.'

She sat up straight, alert.

He said, 'Chronically.'

So. A wife who chronically needed him. A permanent alibi. A fortification of the borders.

'What illness is it?' she asked, thinking with fear of cancer, multiple sclerosis.

'Depression.'

Ah, so. She felt sad then, and a bit resentful, that he felt the need to conjure up an illness in a wife to keep himself safe from her, as though he didn't trust her not to make demands. She saw now why he'd been so reluctant to talk, and she was sad that he made no distinction between her desire to know and understand and the making of demands. She gave a wry sad smile.

He saw her expression. He sat up, serious and intent. 'I don't think you understand. It's clinical depression. It's an illness, incapacitating. She's been suffering for years . . .'

He took her finger now, the one with the wedding-ring, and twisted the ring, that circle of plaits, separate strands forever tangled, and he sighed. 'What a trap . . .'

He looked up. 'It's all so complicated. I do want to tell you. I want you to know it all. I'm writing it down for you. I'm writing a book.'

22

When they went to breakfast in the morning, the proprietor brought them a note. He said, 'Message in the night, Chief,' poking his grease-slicked head out from the sizzling serving-hatch as they came in beneath the felt-tipped sign, DINING ROOM. He handed Dave a scrap of paper, greasy from the frying.

'Proper English Breakfast, Chief?' Proper. As though the Great English Breakfast could redeem the past night's sin.

She asked, 'What is it?' She was imagining with growing horror his wife ill and desperate in the night.

The sun bounced off the Formica and blinded her. He handed it over, and against the light she couldn't at first make it out.

It was garbled and cryptic. It frightened her.

She said, 'Who could it be from?'

Dave smirked, knowing immediately. He said, 'Your nut-case husband.'

She stared in disbelief. But then she saw, yes, the phallic allusion with which the scribbled note ended: *Which one is the biggest and the best?*

A message in the night. A short sharp shock, an aggressive bell, an angry intrusion by one man on another's territory, the relationship, again, seeming to be ultimately between the two men. She felt sick. The grease on her egg wriggled and swam.

Though the message, after all, must surely have been for her. And the proprietor had automatically handed it to Dave.

'Why on earth,' asked Dave, 'Did you tell him where we'd be staying?'

But why not? If someone respected your right to sexual freedom, as Boris had always claimed to, in the past?

'Take no notice,' said Dave, and screwed it up and shoved it in his pocket.

He forked a raw-looking square of sausage through the glaze of yolk. For a gourmet, and for the situation, he seemed, oddly, to relish the food.

It was time to go home. She cleared her things, she picked up her hair-grips that had fallen on the floor. She said, 'They're everywhere, I've been falling apart.'

He said, 'Don't do that, I need you all together for the next time,' but she couldn't smile.

Over lunch in an Italian restaurant, she tried to talk about the way they were obviously hurting Boris. He said, 'There are no rules.' He said, 'You're not going to cry on me, are you?' She cried.

And in the tube the clatter of her heels echoed on the tiles, letting everyone know she was coming, wobbly and vulnerable and unable to flee, letting anyone know, any rapist, any murderer, any man round the archway holding a gun . . . she felt like a victim, the wrong sort of heroine, as though the story they'd started out acting had unravelled out of their control. Which was how she felt also when Dave had come up the stairs and into the room grinning and said, 'Do you know what the proprietor said just now about you? "We get a lot of girls in here, Chief, but not so many of that class." '

('A true professional,' he'd said, coming towards her.)

97

And in the train her back throbbed, as it always did when she'd left him, with unreleased sexual tension, the failure of orgasm.

She thought about Boris's message. She remembered it precisely: *The body politic has many organs. Which one is the biggest and the best?*

She understood what he meant: *The body politic*: he meant the State, and in particular two contrasting types: potential revolutionaries like himself and wet liberals like Dave. And of course it was sexual double-entendre.

But it was a different meaning that had struck her when the letters had wriggled into shape in the sunlight: the word *organ* had danced and buzzed: it was church organs she thought of, and bodily organs depicted in paint. As if someone had found her out.

She'd had a premonition.

23

After that, Dave took to writing to her daily. The letters pierced the letterbox, sharp white strips flicking in like knives.

'He's turned your head,' said Boris, and she thought of the film they'd once seen together, in which the head of a child possessed by a devil turned right round on her neck.

Dave wrote that in response to the news about Johnny he was trying to give up smoking.

('With the money I'd save if I gave up smoking,' he'd once said laughing, 'I'd buy you a crimson satin corset.')

He had started on the book; in addition to all his other writing commitments he was managing five pages a day. He called it *levelling*. He called it *coming clean*.

('Another letter,' said Boris, 'from your dirty old man.')

Dave said he'd taken back the wine-bottle they'd never got round to opening before she'd left the last time, and added: *Empty*; and she had a vision of a genie flown, loose and out of control . . .

She stood at the window in the flat, and watched the leaves unpick themselves from the trees.

My Dearest, Darling, Wonderful Bron,

I write this having just arrived back, in a weekend with a deadline, from, would you believe it, shopping. Two hours ago, Amanda suddenly took it into her head to go and buy some material for curtains, and I must needs drop my work and take her. It's not often she gets enough energy and enthusiasm to do anything like that, and it's important to encourage and support her when she does. In fact, we don't need curtains, and indeed on a writer's pittance can ill afford them, particularly as I'm somewhat behind on my latest BBC commission. It would in fact have been better therefore if she could have found some other reason for getting out of the house, and so, without wanting to push it too far (and keeping off the subject of money, since she is liable to take it as a reproach, her illness now having impaired her earning capacity for years), I say, 'Are you sure? Why do you need to make curtains, we never even draw them out here in the dale?'

She stares at me blankly, and says: 'I just feel like it,' and I know it would be unkind to take it any further.

So we ups and gets in the car, and drives to our nearest market town, and off she goes to the haberdasher's, and I while away the time at the stationer's, buying typewriter-ribbons and white-out and whatnot.

I make my way back to the memorial in the square where we've agreed to meet. Needless to say, I have to wait: her illness makes her incredibly slow. At long last she comes trailing, her hair falling down from its bun, her petticoat drooping, her tights wrinkled, and yet with a kind of dotty hauteur which is pitiful to witness. It breaks my heart, the way her illness has brought so fine a woman, once so proud and confident, so low.

Bron, I know you will not flinch at my writing so openly of my feelings for my wife. As you said, the truth can't hurt us if we don't let it, the truth is better faced. It is better that we level.

I am grieving for Amanda. Yet coping with her is a strain, and I have to confess that I do not always behave very well.

We get home. With her bag of material she trails into the living-room.

I say: 'Well, let's see.'

She fumbles, looking at me with a shiftiness I find incredibly painful. She pulls it out.

It is deep lurid purple.

I say, 'Oh, which room did you want it for?'

She says lamely, 'This one.'

We are in a room with a mustard-yellow carpet.

She looks round forlornly, focusing, making the connection, or rather, the lack of connection. She says weakly, 'It doesn't go.'

She drops the material. She says, 'I don't want to make it after all.'

All our effort wasted, the money spent on the material, the petrol, an afternoon's working-time. That's how it is with her illness: a destructive cycle of lost effort, but effort that, grindingly, just in case it should be fruitful, has to be made.

But what of you, my darling? Have you tackled your husband, Boris, about his very strange and spiteful behaviour in sending that message to our hotel? You really must, you know, as I said in my last letter – you simply can't let him bully you like that.

My darling, I could bear our time apart better, if only you would write . . .

For ever yours,

Dave.

'It wouldn't affect my wife,' he'd said, the last time they'd met, trying to encourage her to write, and she had wondered afterwards precisely what he'd meant. Did he mean that his wife, lost in her depressive daze, would notice nothing, and therefore never guess? Or was it that even if she did guess she wouldn't care, something of what she'd once been, a satirical beauty, would rise up to judge a letter from a husband's passing mistress beneath her contemptuous attention? Could it be, she wondered out of her working-class puritanism, as he called it, that the domestic attitudes and arrangements of the semi-Bohemian middle classes did not lead spouses to wonder about each others' mail?

But of course, it was possible that in any case he'd misjudged; that he was believing what he wanted to, out of desperation (she told herself, giving him the benefit of the doubt), believing what he needed to.

Well, she didn't want a relationship based on deceit. If his wife's knowledge ended her own relationship with him, well, so be it.

It was with this sense of pushing things, testing them out, and also with a pervasive anxiety that she sat down and wrote.

Dear Dave,

. . . . When he rang our hotel Boris was not being as malicious as you think, he just got drunk and lost control. He was simply jealous and lonely, feelings which of course you don't avoid having just because you don't believe in possessiveness. When I got back home, he was full of remorse and shame – indeed, he broke down and wept – and his behaviour on the whole has been remarkably unpossessive: it's very painful, for instance, for him to have your letters arriving here, but he hardly says a thing . . . .

(Perhaps, she felt afterwards, it had been insensitive to write to him so painstakingly defending Boris. But then it was he, Dave, who had so insistently dragged Boris in, demanding she tackle him, assuming authority on

how he should be dealt with, as though he knew about
Boris better than she . . .)

24

As she wrote, she glanced now and then at his letter
and the story of the curtains.

In her head, a different version of the curtain-story
grew.

There was a woman, who was tired and depressed, and
who looked through a window, out across a valley. The
valley was soft, with the melting browns and rusts of
autumn, and as she looked at it, the woman's heart
rose. And she hit on the notion of curtains to draw the
colours of the valley in to her, to enable her, instead of
standing lonely at the edge of things, to hold them
within her room . . .

She thought with a sudden appetite of the satisfying
pock of the needle in linen, and of the soft completed
folds like pillars joining landscape and home.

She went to her husband. She couldn't drive. She
would have to ask him to give up an hour or two's
work to take her to buy material before the shops closed
for the weekend. And so she began at a disadvantage,
in the role of a nuisance.

But her eagerness, and her sudden grip on her right
to fulfilment however brief or trivial, gave her the
courage to pursue it, and to face the objection she knew

he would have: that she was asking him to spend the money which, by giving up the afternoon to take her to town, he'd fail to earn.

The husband did indeed think these things, but he refrained from speaking them, feeling pleased with himself for a forbearance he would later be able to recount to his mistress as he no doubt privately liked to call her, though knowing she wouldn't like it); he merely offered a remark on their lack of need for curtains in the country, for which he could less easily be accused of callousness and contempt.

And the woman saw through him, and rallied with a fine contempt of her own, for his self-deceit, his image of himself as a kind but overburdened man. And she said with a surge of confidence in her own instincts, and her right to express them: 'I just feel like it.'

But she saw how he smirked, and had taken it as stupidity, and her spirit fell in the face of his determined preconceptions. And outside, in the world where he strode loose-limbed, confident and acknowledged as the local (but oh-so-down-to-earth-and-friendly) celebrity, she felt the skin he had cast on her weigh heavy, the stereotype of hag, and her feet dragged as she made her way to the haberdasher's across the square.

And in this shop there was no material like that she'd imagined; of course there wouldn't be – a market town in the hills that he'd brought her to, because that was where he had chosen to write. There were ten rolls only, and none of them suitable.

But, out of defiance, defiance of the barrenness and lack of choice in her situation, she wouldn't go back empty-handed. Out of sudden sheer subversion she bought ten yards of lurid purple, and tucked it under her arm and carried it back across the square under his watching eyes.

And she knew he was appraising her as she walked: dowdy, messy, an appearance born out of utter lack of energy, out of a sense of total stasis, of no future to go on to or to dress up for. And she felt defiant about this, too; almost proud, as she walked, flaunting the evidence of her plight, her state of mind.

And the man noted this, and saw her pride as inappropriate, a sign of madness, though he was of course too discreet to call it that, too aware of the danger of opening himself up to the accusation of making outdated dismissive judgments; he called it illness.

And later he would recount the appearance of his wife to his mistress, as a warning, so that his mistress would not likewise let herself slip, because he was a man who believed in the power of symbols, and was afraid that dislocated clothes could give you a dislocated soul . . .

Back at home, getting the material out of the packing, the woman began to falter under his stony quizzing gaze. Perhaps, she began to feel, after all she had bought the purple cloth out of a simple squalid fear of his scorn if she came back empty-handed. And where had it got her? His scorn could scarcely be colder as he gazed in silence from the purple cloth to the mustard tones of the room. She lost faith in herself, dropping the cloth, standing useless, arms hanging, and his scorn was all the harsher for being unspoken.

But the man saw himself as having been forebearing, though he mentioned later to his mistress his inability at times to behave well; for there might be times after all when he'd have to confess differently. And he felt in all honesty he could congratulate himself for facing up to his weaknesses; he'd done well to confess them.

She knew now that nothing he ever wrote could she trust as the truth in her own terms. No letter, no life-story, no book.

And as she wrote, his wife seemed to enter the room, slipping in through the borders, infusing her life and melting its shape. As though the real relationship now were with her. . . .

She wrote:

> Are you sure your wife's behaviour isn't simply a quite reasonable reaction to her unconfirmed suspicions; i.e. about you and me?

She put the letter in the postbox.

She felt a headache beginning behind her eyes.

> Dear Bron (with a cold little slap the unusually formal address hit her eye),
>
> I am very angry that you should so minimise my wife's serious and disabling illness. To suggest that her behaviour is merely repressed emotional reaction to an exterior circumstance is to do a grave disservice to a woman whose most striking characteristic has always been emotional honesty.
>
> Your evidently very active imagination can nevertheless in no way touch the complexities of the situation my wife and I share. Difficult and acrimonious as our relationship is, we understand each other very

106

well, and no amount of crass observation by a relative stranger can in any way add to our understanding.

She was stung, by the alacrity with which, at the first sign of trouble, he'd closed ranks against her with his wife, by how deftly he'd slipped her from one place into the other: desirable mistress into troublesome other woman.

Well, what else did she expect, seeing through him as she did now, as she should have all along, if some ridiculous need hadn't got in the way? Oh, she may have got the wife wrong (modelled her, no doubt, on her too-passive, too-wavering self), but she'd put her finger on him. Aggressive, touchy, interpreting challenge as mere crude attack, lashing out and alien. He insulted her: *crass observation*, *relative stranger*; and as much as it stung her, she despised him for such a crude childish ploy.

Her heart closed against him.

Well, good. It was simpler to have her heart closed, than messily open, the way it had been. It was cleaner and simpler to be able to despise him.

She wrote:

How dare you suggest that I should want to interfere in your marriage? When, as it seems it is necessary for me to point out, I have one of my own I wouldn't want interfered with?

She posted the letter, hardly expecting a reply.

But one came.

My Darling, Wonderful, Bron,

Your letter brought me to my senses. Your anger was like the lashing out of a wounded animal. I hurt you. Oh, my darling, how could I hurt the one I so love? It so grieves me that I have. I lashed out, too, but coldly, cruelly. This is what they did to us in the army, trained us to hit back the minute we are threatened. Oh, my darling, would that I could divest myself of this male conditioning, this reflex to lash out and kill . . .

My sweet Bron, undeserving as I am, I ask your forgiveness and the opportunity to explain.

I was writing to you, unadvisedly, in the middle of a crisis. One evening last week I decided that the time had come to tell Amanda about you, that I could not go on with the pain of deceit. I went downstairs with this express aim, my heart thudding. It is no easy thing to bring such hurtful truth to someone already laid low by an illness such as Amanda's.

She was sitting in an armchair mending my old dressing-gown, quietly patching holes, the holes that my living had worn. I'm sure you will understand my saying, my darling, that at the sight of her I thought I would not be able to go on, indeed did not want to.

It is not that she would have been surprised to hear that I had been having an affair – you must know, my sweet, that this is something which over the years she has come to expect. Ours has never been a cosy marriage, and Amanda has had affairs of her own; however, in our wild and searching unfaithfulness we have nevertheless understood one another, and we do have a bond it would be painful to break.

No. The fact of mere physical infidelity would not hurt her. But of course this time I had something to tell her that would indeed hurt her deeply: that I had met the woman who had finally brought my search to an end. The woman about whom I could never use the sordid word *affair*; the woman with whom I have found both sexual passion and at long last true love. In short, my dearest, the woman with whom I want to spend the rest of my life.

And of course, the news hurt her, and of course we had a terrible scene, in which all the recriminations and sordid details of the last nineteen years spattered like acid, the whole history of which I am writing in the book, and which has all been a prelude, a quest unfolding itself towards the present, ending, my darling, in you.

And in the middle of it all, your letter arrived, and foolishly, reprehensibly, I immediately replied, out of all that acrimony and anger, wanting to reach out, but with only bitterness and anger to impart, and no conclusion to relay, no sense of where it was all leading, and therefore said nothing of what was happening, leaving you sadly, painfully, in the dark as to the source of my anger and agitation.

But now we do have a conclusion. It is that Amanda is leaving. She is to try her luck in London. She has never really taken to the countryside, and that may well have exacerbated her depression in recent years. A move back to London in fact may well do the trick. It was always on the cards, and the time is ripe, after all: Elspeth recently left for university, so there is no child to keep Amanda here any more. She will stay with her sister, until she gets back on her feet and finds a job. And the beauty of it is that in London she'll receive better psychiatric care.

So, believe it or not, I will soon be alone. How quickly and magically things resolve themselves in the end. I will have to re-learn to cook. There is a delicatessen in our nearest town that sells freshly-ground spices; the owner is an expert, having been posted in Malaysia at the end of the war (which goes to show, I suppose, that good can come out of anything bad) – I'll have to perfect some curries, and then you will have to come and sample. I'll prepare you a feast, my darling, that you won't be able to refuse . . .

It is a load off my mind to have told Amanda, and to have got things moving for the benefit of all of us. I rose this morning with a sense of release and hope. I looked out across the valley drenched with the soft misty sun of early morning, and for the first time in years felt a calm relaxed confidence, knowing that those hills, soft and round as your breasts, join rather than divide us, and that one day you may cross them to me . . .

And I am keeping on with cutting down smoking. I'm down to twenty a day, half of what I was smoking when I started the campaign. It's good to have you to write and tell, it keeps me at it, knowing I've got to report, and knowing that you are caring and willing me to succeed. And – after a little hiatus (it's impossible to work in the midst of emotional turmoil)

– I'm getting on with the book. My BBC commission is suffering, but what the hell; the book, your book, will be finished by Christmas, which is the really important thing.

And also now I am able to turn my attention to a matter that's been troubling me: your husband, Boris. My darling, he has acted very strangely, and I feel he may be ill. Believe me, with all my experience of Amanda's illness, I do know the danger signs. I think you should try and get him to see a doctor. Do write, my darling, and tell me you forgive me. I wait in eager anticipation, loving you more than ever each day.

Dave.

She was horrified. She had a rush of guilty pity, and then a wave of cold anger at his high-handed assumptions and demands.

Oh fine: bundle Boris off to a psychiatrist, that would make it easer – just as he was bundling his wife off to London. So much for that woman's depression, her 'clinical illness'. A convenient label for unhappiness that saved him from having to accept any responsibility for its cause. Miraculously lifting, notice – just enough – when suddenly it was convenient to have her make the effort to clear off out of the way.

Though who wouldn't end up depressed, in her situation? Sentimentally bullied, required to 'patch the holes his living had worn'? Which of course was precisely what he would require of her also; to 'keep him at it', to take responsibility for his giving up smoking; to spend the rest of her life behind him, keeping him alive.

No wonder his wife's depression was lifting: freed at last by another sucker.

26

Dear Dave,

I am very sorry that you have been making assumptions which I'm afraid are mistaken. I cannot come to live with you and if you had only seen fit to discuss your thoughts about it with me, then I should have made that quite clear. I think it is a great shame that you did not, and it is very sad that such a gap in understanding could have occurred between us.

It is a pity that you seem also to have given your wife a picture of our relationship which for me does not represent the reality, and I hope very much that she has not made her decision to leave on the strength of this alone.

I am sorry also that you dismiss as you do the unhappiness our relationship has caused Boris. He is not ill, he is having a normal reaction to a distressing situation.

Since we see things so differently, and have obviously disappointed each other in our expectations, I think it would be better if we stopped corresponding and did not see each other again.

Yours,
Bron.

Dear Bron,

I am afraid it is you who have been making assumptions. I recollect no reference in my letter to our living together in the near future, and I certainly think that that would be most unwise. My wife's decision to leave, I can assure you, has been made on quite different grounds from those you imagine. It is a matter of our private decision about our marriage. Please do not inflate the importance of your own part in it.

Yours,
Dave.

The same trick, turning nasty: Don't flatter yourself, darling. Did he think it would melt her? It closed her even tighter.

Dear Bron,

Your silence has left me desolate. Your coldness, your stern ban on further contact, which oh my darling, you surely cannot mean and yet which chills and frightens me enough to hesitate to write.

I am doing so because I feel the matter of your husband is urgent.

It is natural that you should want to deny that he is ill; I have observed the touching loyalty with which you speak of him. But it is of course hardest to see objectively those to whom we are closest.

He has not exactly had a history of stability. You have reported his predilection for fashions and poses, indeed, disguises, and his adoption of a name that is not his own. It is no accident, of course, that he chose to take up acting. He is a man, it seems, who must live behind a mask, who has a problem confronting reality. You say he never talks about his past. There is no reality, no real person for you to relate to. It is no wonder that at times your sex life with him has been inadequate. And then when, in your need, you turned to me, he failed to react in the way a husband might be expected to. He showed no real anger: passively, he allowed it all to go on, our meetings in London, my letters dropping through his letterbox . . .

If we are not to call it illness, then we must surely call it indifference, we must assume he doesn't care . . .

But no. During our last meeting he finally flips. Rings the hotel in the middle of the night, sends a message that is undoubtedly the ravings of a madman. And finally, when you go home, he breaks down completely and weeps, a man sitting sobbing in a chair . . .

I urge you to get him attention quickly, at least some kind of counselling. Marriage Guidance might do as a start, but watch them, they tend to like to send married couples off into the sunset holding hands. A psychiatric referral from your GP would be preferable.

I realise I may no longer have the right to give you my personal news, but in the hope that you're not going to wipe me out completely I shall dare a little.

I've had a set-back in my Stop-Smoking Campaign but can at least report that I'm back on the ladder again now.

Since her decision to leave, Amanda has given up

the housework completely. She never was a Great Housewife, to say the least, as Elspeth and I know to our cost, but things have gone from bad to zilch, as Elspeth would say. Therefore I must needs take over myself, turning into your actual Eighties Househusband. It's a question at the moment of cutting through the disgusting grime and grease that congealed over everything during her years of slatternly half-management.

Ever yours, should you need me,
Dave.

Dear Dave,

There is no point in your trying to engage in a battle to defeat Boris because you see him as a rival. I do not consider it madness or illness, or whatever you want to call it, to suffer a lover's infidelity without flying into a macho rage. I do not consider it illness or madness in a man to cry. Your attempt to reduce Boris to the role of pathetic victim, i.e. psychiatric patient, is a subtle and pernicious form of the macho fight-to-kill.

Please do not write again. I feel there is nothing more we can fruitfully say.

Bron.

But she'd been unnerved. For instance, was it true that all along Boris just hadn't cared?

Dear Bron.

It is the basest, cruellest, most bone-headed disrespect to dismiss psychiatric patients as 'pathetic victims'. Oh indeed, they *are* victims: of precisely that kind of gross discrimination – both from within the medical profession and, as you so contemptuously illustrate, without.

I can assure you that when I show concern for your husband's mental condition, I am not dismissing him out of hand, sending him into a pigeon-hole where he can be discounted. No indeed, I am treating him with the utmost respect, understanding that, like a man with a heart attack, he needs care and attention to bring him back to the health and freedom he has a right to expect.

I ask you now – no I demand – that while you are still his wife you discharge your duty as one, and bring him to this healing process.

There comes a time for all of us when we need to give up and give in, hand over responsibility for ourselves to others. Physical illness forces us to recognise that ourselves, but in mental illness it is necessary for those around us to recognise it for us. I implore, I insist that you now do this for Boris.

The insanity of a spouse is in fact grounds for divorce, but it would of course be utterly cruel to abandon a partner simply because he is ill. This is why, however, you must do your utmost to get him back on the road to health; to have him free and strong when you do make the break and extricate yourself from a marriage which has trapped and cramped you for so long.

You will of course then be able to quote his behaviour as grounds for mental cruelty – his secrecy, his refusal to communicate, his refusal of sex – all of which have caused a stress of which your headaches are the clearest evidence.

    Yours,
        Dave.

Dear Dave,
    Do not bully me by writing again.
        Bron.

But she was trembling as she posted this. There was a strength of feeling in this last letter of his – oddly displaced into the issue of the status of psychiatric patients – which unnerved her, and which she did not fully understand.

Dear Bron,
    If you won't do something to help Boris, I will. It may interest you to know that David Field is an old BBC pal of mine. I intend to inform him that the substantial part he recently offered Boris would undoubtedly strain Boris to cracking-point in his present state, and suggest that in Boris's own interest the offer should be withdrawn.

    Remember, I have documentary proof of Boris's insanity, the message he sent to our hotel.

    Yours,
        Dave.

Dave –
    I shall not open any further letters you send.
        Bron.

But she was afraid it was too late, that he would be ringing David Field even now . . .

He rang her up.

'Bron?' His voice was thin, a lost sad finger of sound on the distances between them.

She waited, listening.

'You said you loved me. You said you loved me whatever, that it wasn't conditional.'

She couldn't speak; to speak would be to get trapped, to have him twist her words.

'My life is in ruins. My wife has gone. My work is in chaos. I've lost my BBC commission . . .'

The wires pinged as if breaking.

'You've betrayed me.' His voice was suddenly even and cold. 'You've gone back on your word.'

She said, 'Please leave me alone,' and put the phone down.

As she walked away across the room, it rang again, punching the air with short sharp shocks. She sat trembling till it stopped. For a long while after, the air into which it had been ringing seemed still to vibrate.

Days passed. Frost came in the night and turned the leaves black. They fell like dark scales. She waited in trepidation for something awful to happen at the theatre.

Boris said, 'Cool it, do you think David Field would be interested in the opinion of a seedy old hack like him?'

And nothing happened.

She tried to work. She too had got behind with her commissions. She hadn't worked well all summer. There were chances she'd failed to follow up, and the work she'd managed had had no artistic grip, no style. Her present brief to fit an illustration around a square of print wasn't working. The cold block of print, established and pre-eminent, exerted a pressure which angled and contrained the style of her drawing.

In the flat, the clock ticked, like an unexploded mine.

One day the doorbell rang. She opened the door and a crew-cut delivery-man pushed a bunch of roses towards her, dark red roses, the colour of the one Dave had planted for her.

'Your lucky day!' said the messenger, rolling his eyes and raising his eyebrows.

Like a practical joker.

No message.

She threw them quickly in the bin.

A letter thudded through the door. It lay on the mat, the usual white envelope, but this time bulging and inscribed *Urgent*. It throbbed in the sunlight.

She picked it up. She put a line through her own address, crossing herself out of his life. She wrote his address at the side.

She posted it back unopened, cutting him off, out of her life.

But as it dropped heavily into the box, she was left with a sense rather of having released something dangerous, a piece of knowledge she needed; she'd let it free and out of her control.

The leaves dropped; the air was still, the trees fell apart slowly, there was no quick clean ending. She grieved, for the fact that he'd treated her so viciously.

In the yard down below the roses stuck out from under the lid of the dustbin. They'd gone brown, and then in the frost black, but they'd retained perfectly their shape of plump round buds. As if the life in them, though gone rotten, refused to be exorcised.

27

Seeing Boris put on his jacket, and knowing he had no rehearsal, she asked, 'Where are you going?'

She felt shy, and guilty, turning to him for comfort over the events which had so hurt him. He'd be justified in turning round and asking her what business it was of hers. He could stare in hostility and not even answer. Or use her appeal to trap her.

He did none of these things. He said matter-of-factly, almost cheerily, 'I'm off to buy new boots.'

So down to earth, so back-to-basics. Life goes on. Her spirits lifted. She said, 'Can I come?'

'Sure,' he said, perfectly friendly, hardly surprised: no emotional pressure at all.

She got her coat, and they went out into the white winter sunlight together, and she linked her arm through his, and he didn't mind, he neither flinched nor took advantage by drawing her closer, just a casual gesture, as though they'd never stopped doing it all along. And here they were, on their old adventure, going out to buy clothes, dressing up, a bit of a light-hearted game. As though what had happened had been merely a hard-luck patch, or an illness, that he accepted as something they had been through together, and that made no difference in the end.

She held his arm tighter, full of affection for such generosity.

But when they got to the crowds, they were jostled apart, and holding his arm, she fell behind, her body contorted like a wedding-gown mannequin, and she had to let go; and when she said as they walked, 'He didn't contact David Field?' and in response he stopped and turned and said (with oh yes, wonderfully comfortable confidence and humour): 'Look, do you think anyone wouldn't see through that soggy old menopausal hack?' – well, then she couldn't feel comforted, because it implied such stupidity on her part, and also such waste, it left no crumbs of hope that there had been a point, however thwarted, in embarking on the experience at all. If that's all it had been, a crude cliché you could laugh at, then for what was she suffering this feeling of breaking apart, this seeping sense of decay?

She shivered in the shadow on the corner where they'd stopped.

And then they descended to the basement of the Army Surplus stores, where a smell rose up, dark and musty, which Boris said was the smell of damp walls, and where helmets hung in nets like dead clams, dredged up from the trenches, and knives glittered on the walls.

Boris rummaged in a box. ITALIAN, EX-ARMY, SLIGHTLY SOILED. He put a boot on. He clicked the heel: his ankle flicked, glittering and slim in the row of buckled straps. She felt a sexual stirring. But then he lifted his heel and she saw red Italian mud caught in the

121

almost-new tread, and she knew what the smell was: old sweat gathering mould, the smell of bodies now gone, and she knew that all the games were deadly, and all of them were dancing, soiled, in dead men's shoes.

28

'In this society,' said Boris, 'we need to develop a healthier attitude to death,' clattering in the kitchen in his ex-Italian-army boots. He did a little tap-dance, he did a quick Charlie Chaplin side-kick.

That night she had a dream in which another letter arrived, and as she watched, the words began to wriggle, turning into worms that crawled on the sheet. And then the paper became linen, and the worms were eating and crawling their way through it, and she lifted it and there was a body beneath it, in tweeds and leather patches: Archibald P. Hawfield.

'Cheer up,' he said.

She said, 'I think I might go and stay with my mother.'

He looked surprised, but he passed no comment, he seemed after a moment or two to think it a good idea.

And she thought then, more hopefully: He's changed; this experience has changed us; it has made us more tolerant and generous.

She went home.

Everything seemed to have shrunk: the garden a brief

strip with a few scrawny trees; the house, a few widths of brick borrowed from a length of terrace. This was the haven that she'd had to come back to, that she'd once imbued with such powers of detention that she'd kept away; this was the place where her mother had kept vigil in case her father ever deigned to return, a scraggy plot in an alien land, that the bulldozer could wipe out in half a day.

Her mother seemed to have shrunk; her hair had shrivelled to grey. She embroidered with a magnifying glass, as though the stitches, silks and needle had all shrunk, the whole world grown too small to handle.

'Three years since you've been,' said her mother, though mildly, without the resentment she'd always sensed in the past.

And she hardly knew her brother, a grown man she'd gone on remembering as a child. And her sister of course absent, living with a man way up north, become a person she hardly knew, and like herself, irrelevant here now, or of only mild affectionate interest.

She told her mother what had happened.

Her mother seemed baffled, as though she couldn't relate the story to the daughter she knew. 'Well,' she said, somewhat sharply, 'you'd better stick with Boris now.'

And later: 'Better the devil you know than the devil you don't know.'

And also: 'It's a terrible thing to break up a marriage.'

Stale crumbs, no comfort.

Like Hansel and Gretel, she'd followed the trail home, but the cold grey pebbles hadn't led to comfort.

She went back, towards London.

123

As the train sped, the pale winter fields flew away and skidded. She was following a path now where the crumbs had been eaten, and she didn't know what devil was waiting at the end of it.

29

The flat was empty. There was two days' mail on the mat. Boris must have been away. Yet he had no reason, he was rehearsing locally. Where could he be?

With half an eye she looked at her mail.

Dear Ms Hawfield, We should be glad of the preliminary sketches you undertook to send us by the end of November. . .

Dear Ms Hawfield, I write to inform you that as you have now failed to meet our extended deadline . . .

The phone rang. She ran, it would be Boris saying where he was.

A voice hissed in her ear. 'You'll get your eyes gouged.' She froze.

'You'll get your skull smashed. You'll get your brains skinned clean. Be ready for a stab in the guts.'

The voice was Dave's.

He said, in a more normal voice, 'Recognise it?'

She forced herself to speak: 'No.'

Sarcastic: 'You don't? Listen to the next bit: This young painter's work is a cultural disembowelling, turning our artistic expectations inside out.'

He waited, and then continued, heavily conversational:

'I'm surprised you missed that one. One of your more florid notices, I think, though admittedly in a minor magazine.'

She said faintly, 'How did you find out?'

He laughed. 'Come on now. It wasn't exactly difficult. Just a matter of getting Clive to press a few buttons.'

It had all been forgotten, but now the computers had released it, like a genie.

He said, suddenly quietly threatening: 'Does Boris know?'

Why did her lungs now batter her rib-cage like a sheet in a storm? What did it matter, all that, compared with what had happened since? And when she and Boris had come through, together? And how did he guess that Boris hadn't known?

He said meaningfully: 'Jason Fulbright. Know the name?'

And now she identified the sting in his voice: sexual jealousy. And she knew what he was assuming: sexual secrecy; he reduced it all to a sordid sneaky undeclared affair. And he didn't like it.

He said, 'You never told me. And there was I, sitting up writing night after night to give you the whole truth about me – and because of which, my work suffered, my career, my professional credibility. All for you. And all the time you never said a word about this. You never came clean.'

Her lungs stuck fast as another thought struck her: How could any of them have made the connection between Bronwen Hawfield and Guinevere Knight?

He said, cutting into her silent wondering, 'Let me tell you how we discovered the connection . . .'

He could read her mind. He could uncover everything, see right through her skin to her throbbing trembling guts and the workings of her mind. The inside story. There was nothing she could hide, yet there was nothing he would understand.

'When I first met you I was eager to know everything about you. Clive would look out copies of all the books you'd illustrated and send them to me . . .'

He'd never said.

The night she met him he'd looked at the cover and plucked out a secret of her soul. . . . She thought of them, two men seeking out her work, not in the expectation of discussing it with her, but for the purpose of monitoring her. And meeting her in London, and neither saying anything, just tacitly monitoring her and dissecting her between them.

He had paused. He was going on, mock-conversational once again. 'Well, it so happened that a book containing some early illustrations of yours had been edited by Don Ellis, an old friend of ours from Cambridge days, whom we hadn't seen for donkeys' years. This prompted us to call him up and invite him to lunch at our club, and over a decent meal and a couple of bottles of Valpolicella, we talked about old times and also jogged his memory about you. One thing he remembered was that for some mad reason' – here he spoke with heavy irony and briefly paused – 'you'd decided to stop using your maiden name and change to your married one, which he'd found odd at a time when most married women were doing quite the opposite.

126

'But the really interesting thing was: a couple of nights later Clive and I were drinking with another old mutual friend of the three of us, and we mentioned our recent meeting with Don and, in the way of things, got talking again about you, and Clive took out the copy he'd acquired of a children's book illustrated by Bronwen O'Donald.' (Another pause. Meaningful, carefully censorious, as if he were catching her out at the back of the class, and calling her up to the front to own up.) 'And then this journalist pal of ours who is present says that he remembers that name, and then recalls that she was the woman he'd once followed when his chum Jason Fulbright was exhibiting some paintings she'd done. It seems she was posing under another name then: Guinevere Knight.' He spat the name, letting it settle.

'For some reason she kept herself very much to herself. Not very keen to show her face in public, it seems . . .' (pause again; the wires clanged) ' . . . indeed practically shrouding herself, apparently. According to my friend Guy Bonder – '

He waited, for this name too to sink; then lightly: 'Ring any bells . . .?

'Well as I say, according to Guy, once the gimmick had worn off, something of a wash-out in publicity terms.'

Carefully: 'It seems she has the habit of standing people up . . . and choosing the worst times to do it.'

Another pause, while time ticked by in the room.

'She stood Fulbright up the night he'd planned a publicity event around her paintings, and it seems he never saw her again. Guy Bonder, having followed her once before and knowing where she hung out in a seedy

127

block of Islington flats, went round to find out why she'd failed to show up. He went in through the entrance hall – one of those dreary council places, all covered in graffiti – and he was about to climb the stairs when she came out of her own door in a raincoat and headscarf and carrying a shopping-bag, for all the world an ordinary dumpy housewife.

'Well, he tracked her for a bit, and discovered who she was: just another minor illustrator skulking round the publishing-houses with her tatty portfolio, and of course he lost interest.

'By the time he mentioned her again to Fulbright she seemed to have disappeared altogether, and Fulbright had cut his losses, understanding that he'd been wasting his effort and time on a project without any future.

'I met him, actually. Guy Bonder introduced us. We had a steak in the club. He's a simpering little ponce, I must say, but I do sympathise with his resentment at how you wasted his effort and time . . .'

Silence; then deadly serious:

'Men don't like it when it turns out that women haven't been honest . . .'

Something caught on the line, a short sharp buzz.

'It seemed that this . . . Guinevere Knight . . . never even came back to collect the money still owing her on the paintings sold. It seems she never even cashed the cheque she'd already received.'

He stopped. 'I wonder why? Perhaps she had something to be ashamed of. Perhaps there was someone she wouldn't want finding out . . .'

And of course she had, of course there was: it was

how she'd seen it all herself, painting as adultery, a sordid sneaky affair.

She said, 'You can't blackmail me,' and put the phone down.

It didn't ring again, although she expected it to, it simply throbbed in the sunlight like a fat black cat.

And she felt weak, with the force of the hatred it seemed to exude at her, all that hatred and bitterness from the world of men, hatred and contempt, for being talented, for being untalented, for being beautiful, for being plain, for being extraordinary, for being ordinary. Whatever she did, whatever she was, she could not escape their contempt; there they were, with their little black books, cooking up versions of her they'd be justified in hating, tucked away in their men's club, their male witches' coven. The Old Boy network, a world of contacts and values of a time before her own, of a class she didn't belong to, they'd fished her out with it, dragged her up, left her stiff like a whale, or a dead body from the Thames, the inside story, her guts exposed.

A world of the past, but all too present; it would always go on. Even Jason, her junior, was of it: it was the network of men.

She had said to her mother: 'Do you know, when I was little I thought Dad was a spy. I was really disappointed to discover that all he was writing in his little book was insurance payments, and not deadly secrets.'

Her mother had replied: 'Oh, it was secrets, all right. Your Dad was in the Masons.'

She'd been shocked. She'd said afterwards: 'Freemasonry, it stinks.'

129

Her mother had laughed. 'It's just overgrown boys playing games.'

The phrases Dave had read out hissed in her head. *You'll get your skull smashed, your eyes gouged.*

Her paintings had been an expression, an exposure of herself, all her meanings and associations laid bare. A vulnerability. But they had taken it as violence.

And violence could be avenged.

In the sun, the phone bulged, a black animal about to spring to life.

Dave had said to her, 'Where've you been half my life?' For almost half his life she'd been unborn, not yet existent. But all hers he'd been alive and lurking, and for some of it much nearer than she'd known, a friend of Guy Bonder's, a friend of people who'd employed her; waiting for her, his Holy Grail. And he'd go on, he'd be out there always, ready to pounce.

She ran from the flat, in search of Boris because she couldn't bear to be alone.

30

At the theatre no one knew where Boris was.

'Try Mortia's,' said a young man materialising beside her in sneakers, chewing gum, and then gone in an instant, trained to do anything, silently and seamlessly.

'What?' she said helplessly, to the young woman sitting smoking in the gloomy depths of the foyer.

'Mortia's Crypt.'

It was a theatrical suppliers and second-hand clothes shop. The familiar musty second-hand smell. Fifties clothes, lots of man-made satin vamp. On the walls, Dracula posters and hand-written notices, part advert, part joke: FOR THAT CRYPTIC LOOK: WHITE PAN-STICK. . . .IN OUR BLACK SATIN SKI-PANTS YOU'LL MAKE A KILL!

The shop was empty, the only movement a girl behind the desk with a white-painted face and her hair in jet-black fright-spikes, putting fish-net gloves on severed alabaster hands.

She turned to go.

At that moment, there was a commotion at the back, someone clattering down stairs and into the shop. She turned.

Boris stood, bent, as though rivetted in mid-jump. He looked astounded, and then, as if with resignation, he relaxed. He leant against the doorframe. From behind him stepped a woman.

The woman placed herself beside him, and Boris folded his arms, and the two of them seemed to compose themselves together. And the woman was wearing a black satin dress with a deep white arrow of cleavage and a slit up the side that showed a glimpse of black stocking and suspender. And a hand rested on the black satin hip, and the nails were deep red.

And the woman caught her gaze, and knew, in the way that female lovers of husbands always seem to, that this was the wife, and shifted, and moved subtly closer to Boris, and Boris, with the slightest movement

131

of his body, accommodated her, and the woman sent a look of smouldering challenge you'd never expect this side of a nineteen-fifties celluloid.

31

You've gone against everything you ever stood for. It was what he had said to her.

I've always wanted to fuck a girl with blood-red fingernails, he had said, swinging round on the Ferris Wheel, coming round full circle.

She felt defeated by the stereotypes. Temptress, vamp. However much she told herself that Boris's woman was underneath no doubt as vulnerable as anyone, she couldn't believe it. Some women could carry off the stereotypes better than others, some women saw fit to use them – however ironically, they nevertheless used them. Just as they could use them pathetically to lure away a sexist father twenty years ago, they could use them now, in these feminist days cynically, to lure away a husband who counted himself ideologically sound. It was worse, because now they could pretend it was a game.

She felt: the old images were too powerful, they exerted a force that affected reality. She was afraid.

Boris left, to live with his woman. He came back for his things.

As he emerged from the bathroom, carrying all his

toilet gear, they trapped each other in the corridor. They shifted, they got stuck again in each other's way. It was dark, the light was behind him, she couldn't see his face. Something clicked in his hand. She daren't look down; it flashed through her mind that it must be the barber's razor he'd once had a craze for.

The moment passed; they stood back, they let each other go. But she trembled, watching his back disappear round the archway of the landing.

She lived alone. She had no work. She'd lost the faith of her publishers. She wrote requesting commissions; she was turned down.

She didn't sleep. She had very little appetite. Alone in the house, she felt breathless and tired.

She went out to sign on for the dole. Half-way there she felt giddy, the buildings reeled, and she had to sit down on a bench.

She stayed at home, writing letters for work, dragging her eyes across the pages of books whose contents she could not afterwards remember, staring blankly at the flickering television screen.

Once a month at least, for three whole days, a splitting headache grounded her, drove her down to the ground.

She thought perhaps the Pill in part was to blame. But to stop taking it because Dave had gone from her life would be to acknowledge too conclusively that she had been taking it for him, rather than creating a choice for herself.

She went on taking it.

And aspirins, to dull the headaches.

And hardly any food.

She had pins and needles in her legs.

As if someone was sticking them into her effigy.

Now and then, she felt a numbness in her left, her painting, hand.

On Christmas Eve, with a half-bottle of whisky that someone had once bought for Boris, she sat in gradually woozy isolation as the screen flickered images of garish family jollity.

Families. She wondered how her mother and brother were celebrating Christmas together: her brother down the pub, perhaps, while her mother stuffed their modest chicken for two. Her sister: what was her Christmas like? She realised she had no idea.

She had a better, clearer picture of Dave's: gourmet sauces for the goose, she thought, the whisky starting to cheer her into satisfying bitchiness; and for the gander – no doubt the wife would be there, back home now his sordid brief affair was over; there'd be fires and tangerines and a daughter home from university holding up the mistletoe for Mum and Dad to kiss each other better. A traditional Christmas, to celebrate the traditional structure resurrected.

She poured herself another drink, bitterly satisfied, satisfactorily sardonic, and raised her glass to the TV screen, and to the bareness of the room, its functional ugliness that had been encouraged, indeed dictated, by Boris, who no doubt this very minute was celebrating amidst decadent purple satin and flickering candles, with probably bloody miniature silver coffins hanging off the tree.

She almost laughed, she swayed, she started crying instead, and flopped across the chair-arm, grabbing the cardi she'd thrown off because the whisky had made her sweat, and flinging it over her head.

She sobbed a long time. When she stopped, there was another, similar sound in the air. A forlorn whooping sound, like someone else wailing. She sat up; the room tipped. Her vision blurred. A finger of rationality pointed out that the sound was in fact that of piped carols, some kind of collection in the street below, and she rose to go to the window to see.

She never got to the window. There was someone standing before it. Gaunt and grim, a skinny woman with dark-shadowed eyes and a shawl about her head. Guinevere Knight. In the flesh.

She passed out.

In the morning she woke to find herself crumpled at the base of the full-length mirror, her cardi round her head, the TV set still whining in the room.

But she'd been visited by a ghost.

At last, in January, she had an offer that at one time she'd have refused, to design the cover for a guide to sexual technique in the age, as the author put it, of the Liberated Woman. How to manhandle a woman who's on fifteen thousand a year, he quipped, then straightened his face and explained that manhandling, actually, wasn't the order of the day any more, folks, it was all-over body contact, a new technique that could make men even quicker on the draw.

She flinched.

(It was she, wanting Dave to tell about himself, who'd said, 'Shoot.')

A variation on Eve's apple, the art editor had asked for.

Dave had written: *I kept the apple you couldn't eat because of your headache. It sits on my desk, cool and round as your breasts.*

She'd said later, 'Apples wither.'

'Not before I eat it.'

She'd said, 'Ouch.'

She worked away, but nothing worthwhile came. Rows of useless sketches, rows of bitter green apples that never would ripen.

She felt breathless, claustrophobic.

She went and opened the window.

The cold wind entered, snatching, and she banged it shut again quickly.

32

A woman rang her whom she'd once met briefly when they'd both contributed illustrations to a children's anthology.

She was surprised, immensely touched, that the woman should even remember her.

Would she like to take part in an exhibition of women's illustrations a group of them were setting up?

She went to the planning meeting. Her headaches started to clear.

The preparations filled her time. The work of the other women stirred her; it was daring in technique and bold in design. She began to feel inspired.

After the exhibition, her own work was more adventurous. And with Boris gone, and all the space to herself, she could turn the flat into a studio and house more bulky and innovative materials; and having learnt from the other women, she started doing wood-cuts and collages. And now she got work again, this time in more amenable, feminist markets.

She began going to meetings. She was invited to join a group organising a festival of women's arts.

They drifted around her, these six or seven other women, some in long dresses with gold-hoop ear-rings, others with their hair chopped and wearing dungarees. They shared a soft discreet manner which, though it soothed her, was nevertheless alien; she missed the grim and almost violent understanding, only half-spoken, which was her only experience with other women.

'We need to develop a female aesthetic,' said these women, modulated as governesses presiding over tea.

Some disagreed (almost): 'It's difficult, though. There's this whole question of whether there's really such a thing as a female imagery.'

There was no real pain in their discussions; and it was this that she didn't understand. They filled her with unease because they seemed emotionally strange. Like the hands of a gentle governess, their words stroked her, but did nothing about the pain inside. She was shy of the lesbianism of some of them, and its general acceptance, it was an emotional mechanism she simply didn't know, but which they believed was open to every woman if she only got in touch with it; and so she felt incomplete and unworthy.

And therefore, still, she kept herself to herself, going out to meetings, but coming back at night to what she thought of as her real world, her little flat where she lived alone with her memories and her fears.

There was one woman called Eleanor, to whom after a time she was drawn in particular – plainer-spoken than most, and with a cool but slightly irritated way of knocking down pretensions.

'That was crap,' said Eleanor mildly, at the end of one particularly long-winded planning meeting, and there was a sense of her having broken a golden rule.

Eleanor was a graduate student who lived with her boyfriend and several others in a so-called communal household. 'It's crap,' said Eleanor, 'the women do the housework while the men go off to their anti-sexism meetings. When we complain they accuse us of being conditioned to impracticable standards, of having an unrealistic idea of how much housework needs to be done!'

She and Eleanor and some other women formed a consciousness-raising group. They sat in a circle on the floor, and over the weeks told each other the para-phrased stories of their lives.

They said things like: 'Right now I'm putting my energies into balancing my work and home life. . .'

And: 'Right now Giles and I feel we have to structure

our relationship in a way that gives us both as much freedom as possible . . .'

And about the other women with whom their men, like all the sexist men down the ages before them, were sleeping: 'Right now I'm working on getting to know Angela independently of Giles, so that she and I can work out what's going on there, psychologically-speaking, I mean, and possibly gain things instead of allowing the whole thing to become destructive . . .'

Sometimes they reminded her of how she had been about Dave's wife. Sometimes it seemed to her that they succeeded where she'd failed, in creating bonds between women over the heads of shared male lovers, but at other times it seemed that by getting rid of the need for subterfuge, they simply made it easier than ever for men to help themselves off every plate going.

Sometimes the way they talked reminded her of Boris.

Above all, they were blandly articulate in a way that, as far as she knew, the middle classes always had been; they'd just found some new words to express their old habit of wanting to structure the world.

Oh, they had their Utopia: a world in which emotion had been reasoned out of existence; and the prospect frightened and depressed her, but in any case, she didn't believe in it.

Of course, Eleanor was different. 'This is crap,' she said. 'I can't stand all this sitting around talking about men.' And left, and simultaneously moved out of the bed she shared with her boyfriend and into that of another woman.

And, the initial balance spoilt, the group broke up, almost, it seemed in the end, before it had got going.

So much for sisterhood, she thought, and felt grimly vindicated, but also depressed.

The pressure started up again behind her eyes. The headaches returned.

Eleanor brought cake.

Eleanor's getting quite homey, she thought.

Eleanor said, 'Get back in touch with femaleness, with the womanly bond.'

Eleanor said, 'Go and see your mother.'

But at her mother's she saw her brother as an aggressive colonising male, his height and strength almost frightened her, she bristled when he came into the room calling, 'Is there a cup of tea?'

'Get it yourself,' she said, too sharply, with too much of a challenge, and he bristled also, and henceforth there was a state of angry resentment between them.

And her mother, sensing trouble, panicking and upset, rushed to the teapot, to resurrect the normal order, and poured a cup of tea for him.

'Honestly, Mam,' she said afterwards, when he'd gone, 'a grown man like him.'

But her mother had closed to her, taking her brother's side, knowing where her bread was buttered, appeasing the one appointed by brute strength and convention to change her plugs and fix the toaster and chase away the other men, the burglers and rapists who might come banging on the door at night.

And she felt angry with her mother, and betrayed by her, and also she felt contemptuous, knowing now how Eleanor felt.

Although after that she started going back more often.

33

Time passed. A year, and then another.

Eleanor quarrelled with her lover, and then made it up again. She seemed none the worse for wear. 'Relationships with women don't take it out of you like relationships with men,' she said, in a mood of advocacy.

But from the outside there seemed little difference: Eleanor now was part of a couple, out of which, however close their previous friendship, Eleanor could now only be borrowed. More so: there was missing that feeling of subversive conspiracy of heterosexual women alone together away from men.

Eleanor got tougher, more impatient:

'You need to make an effort to help yourself. Do something about your situation. Move in with us, we're an all-women household now.'

'But I'd rather live alone.'

Eleanor didn't believe her, thought it perversity, a manipulation for attention.

She wondered herself why it was that she clung to her loneliness. She was too old and too used to it, too accustomed to an old emotional groove to make a change without too much pain.

Eleanor, ten years younger, called it simple lazy

141

cowardice. Eleanor accused her of prejudice; Eleanor called her ageist.

She thought of her own impatience, once before, with Dave.

When once she'd seen with pleasure Eleanor's bushy head crossing the road below towards the building, she now reacted with a certain dread, a sense of unwanted pressure.

'Look,' said Eleanor one day, 'you can't go on thinking of that terrible man, that Dave. You can't go on living in dread of him.'

It was true. It was what she was doing. She started to cry. Eleanor held her, rocked her.

'That shit,' murmured Eleanor, stroking her hair.

'Don't say that,' she said, drawing away. 'Just like Boris. When you dismiss him like that you dismiss me.'

Eleanor was angry, irritated. 'What the fuck are you talking about? Of course I dismiss him – as if by his actions he didn't dismiss his bloody self – but why the fucking hell does that dismiss you? Why the fuck can you only see yourself in relation to men?'

She said, recovering a little, 'I thought feminists didn't say fuck.'

Eleanor banged her fist on the arm of the chair. She seemed unaccountably upset. She said, 'Look. Forget about men.'

'I already did that, Eleanor, once before. In my teens, after my Dad left. But men jumped out again, I couldn't stop them.'

Eleanor groaned: 'It's different, now lesbianism's a more acceptable option.'

142

She looked at Eleanor, whose face was aflame, with protest, with some kind of defensiveness. Could it be true – was it simply that Eleanor was doing now what she herself had done then, repressing the need to acknowledge the unpalatable existence of men, and simply had more concrete and socially acceptable ways of keeping up the pretence?

Or could it be that, had she herself grown up in a different time, a different climate, she'd have had a different emotional option that would have set her life on entirely different paths?

She didn't know; she had no way of knowing.

She couldn't tell anything, she had no way of knowing if she was seeing things straight. At her mother's, her brother asked her, 'Cup of tea?' the teapot poised, offering, and his manner was bright and artificial and strained, he could almost be taking the piss. But maybe he really was trying to be pleasant, and if so, was he doing it cynically, diplomatically, for her mother's sake, or was it his own sincere attempt to make amends? Had she judged him unfairly?

'Don't you remember,' said her mother, when he'd gone, as if reading her thoughts, 'what a funny little boy he was? So timid, always being bullied. He can be a bit arrogant at times, but I think it's a kind of nervousness, a compensation.'

Her mother smiled. 'Remember how scared he was of going to school? I suppose it was being brought up in a house full of women.'

She bit her tongue. She didn't say: Why blame women for everything that's ever wrong with men?

Instead she said, to try and sort out two confusions at once: 'Do you think he's like Dad?'

There was a silence.

Her mother took her specs off and looked at her sharply. 'He'd have a job, since he isn't even his son.'

What was this?

The story changing shape . . .

Her mother sighed: 'Well your Dad never really came to terms with a baby that wasn't his own. We tried to make it work. We'd both been guilty. We moved, to start again and try and forget everything that had happened, on either side. But there was always the boy there to remind him. It wasn't all that long before he started going back to see her.' As always, she empha-sised the 'her' as if unable to bring herself to give the woman the dignity of a name or a particular identity, and as usual, although she'd only ever spoken of her rarely, it had the curious paradoxical effect of elevating her, the other woman, to mystical proportions.

But something had shifted.

It was easier for him, of course; much harder for a woman, having to carry the evidence of transgression. And contemptible of him to hold that against her.

Even so, she could no longer see her mother as the chaste and blameless one. The balance had changed.

The needle pocked in the tautened cloth. Practised stitches. Familiar facts, but with unfamiliar significance. . .

'There were a couple of times when he tried to give her up altogether. One of those times she came to the flat in the middle of the night with things he'd left at her place and threw them all against the flat door. You kids woke up, but luckily then she went away.'

Noises on the landing. For years afterwards, they'd thought it was a ghost.

Her mother said of her brother, 'The point is, it made it so difficult for him, growing up with your Dad feeling about him like he did. It made him neurotic. He was scared of everything, scared of spiders, scared of aeroplanes flying over in the sky. But now of course he has to be the way men are expected to be. He has to try and fit in.'

It was easier if things fitted. A category for everything, a set place in the scheme of things, like a genus in Biology, nothing you couldn't put your finger on.

Victim, Culprit. They were shifting from their categories, her mother and her father, straddling the categories, one shoe off, one shoe on.

Her mother said, 'He had a cheek,' and her tone was shot with affection, the strain of bitterness wasn't pure.

Something lit in her memory: like a bright spot appearing, a recessive gene emerging, on the petal of a pea.

He had a cheek.

It was a bright summer day. They were riding in the car, just her and her father. She was five. They were off on her father's insurance round. He was taking her with him, this time he wasn't leaving her behind.

145

Green trees flickered. He drove one-handed, tapping a cigarette on the wheel. They came towards a hump-backed bridge, he shoved the fag between his teeth, and as they went over he shouted 'Whee!' She was laughing, she was holding her stomach to try and stop it flying, she was holding her sides.

And then they stopped beside a cottage. 'Watch this,' he said, grinning, showing his teeth with the fag pushed between them, pushing back his hat like the gangsters in films, they were gangsters together, she would like to do this always, and never go home.

He got out. He sauntered, hands in pockets, his jacket bunched like a cocky tail, towards the cottage he was meant to visit as a respectable businessman.

And then he flew: leaping, and leaping again now, out of her memory: one-handed, over the wall, the rest of him swivelling on one thin strong wrist, and then dropped neatly, in the flower-bed, a place where you weren't supposed to stand.

34

It was late autumn, a hot day when it ought to have been wintry. On the wall, down below the kitchen window of her flat, two cats basked in the sun. Cats, changers of shape, just now two fat cushions, this side of the boundary.

She felt breathless. In the flat, the air was still, heated

through the glass. Unseasonable. Dust-motes hardly moved, as if caught in a time-warp.

She wasn't working very well. She breathed in deeply; she sighed.

A letter dropped onto the mat. It was addressed in a round, unfamiliar hand.

Dear Bron,

It will perhaps seem strange to you to receive this kind of letter from someone you hardly know and indeed have never met. However, I feel I know you very well, and know that you are simply too generous and good to just dismiss it.

Since you left Dad, over three years ago now, he has been in a terrible state, and things have got to a stage where something has to be done, and I could think of no way but to write to you.

THIS IS NOT AN EMOTIONAL BLACKMAIL LETTER – PLEASE READ ON!

I am writing entirely of MY OWN ACCORD – in fact, when I suggested it to Dad he begged me not to, as he doesn't want to PUT ANY EMOTIONAL PRESSURE ON YOU AT ALL.

I am NOT asking you to start loving him again, that would be quite preposterous; when love is dead it's dead, and there's nothing that can be done about it, and there's no point in trying to apportion blame, as Dad says.

The trouble is, though, Dad can't forget you, and the point is if he's going to be happy he needs to. And the reason he can't forget you is that he can't *understand*. He simply doesn't know why you gave

147

him up. You did it so abruptly, and without any explanation, and that does indeed seem strange for someone so caring and good-hearted as you. He just can't get it out of his mind that really you loved him just as much as ever, but that you simply couldn't cope, and maybe succumbed to pressures from your husband. And so he goes on, grieving and hoping, when really he ought to be putting it all behind him and starting again.

As he says, it's really hard to come to terms with something if you don't know what the terms are.

There must, I am sure, be a very good reason for why you acted as you did, though I do sometimes wonder if his idea of it is right.

It would be too much, I suppose, to expect you to write to him and give him the explanation he needs, but I wonder if you and I could perhaps meet? As you see, I live in London, and we could perhaps meet for a coffee one afternoon. If I could understand, I might be able to resolve it once and for all.

Please do answer my plea! Things are really so desperate – Dad is really so low, I'm very afraid of what might happen. I love my father so much, and I do so want to make him happy and well. I have already left it far too long before doing anything, being too busy with a silly minor breakdown of my own – over stupid things like not having a boyfriend, and finding the work at university miles above me (I gave the course up – I'm doing a secretarial course now!) – and I didn't realise the seriousness of what was happening to poor old Dad stuck up there in Yorkshire all alone.

Hoping desperately to hear from you,
    In love and friendship,
        Elspeth.

She showed the letter to Eleanor.

'Bloody crap,' said Eleanor. 'He's set her up to it, obviously.'

She shivered. That night, winter set in. The cats, out on the cold roof, wailed for hours on end.

'But,' she said to Eleanor, 'I guess I did owe him an explanation.'

'We don't owe men anything, least of all an explanation!'

'Then how can they change, if they don't ever know what they're doing wrong?'

'Give me strength! They can work it out for their fucking selves!'

But how? She remembered the helpless feeling that her explanations would have no meaning for him, that her words would have broken like reeds against his different understanding.

She said, 'It's airless in here.'

Eleanor said, 'I find it rather cold.'

As though the cold were squeezing oxygen out of the air.

'Bloody great, isn't it?' said Eleanor. 'Who'd have thought we were over a decade into the women's move-ment – young women like that still running round picking up the pieces for men and doing their bloody dirty work.'

She pondered. *A minor breakdown of my own . . .*

not having a boyfriend . . . I gave the course up . . . This young woman was under stress; these weren't causes but effects.

Outside, the wind got up, and the moon through the window suddenly seemed to race.

She felt angry with Dave; or perhaps, more, a certain horror.

She said, 'Elspeth needs to be shown she's being used by him.'

Eleanor sneered. 'Some women are beyond it. Those who go that far, pressuring other women for men.'

Of course the moon was still, it was the clouds that were racing. It shone, distant and cold, yet sending currents of force across the black space to earth.

She said, 'I think I'll go and meet her.'

In the cafe where she'd written that she'd wait, nobody came. No blonde girl, as Dave had described her, came through the door and stood looking round for her.

She waited an hour, then paid the bill and left.

'What did I tell you?' said Eleanor, almost triumphant.

'Perhaps I just picked a night she couldn't make it . . .'

'So why didn't she write and let you know?'

Nothing happened. She heard no more.

35

The headaches came with a vengeance, a force that pressed behind her eyes and throbbed in a seam along the right side of her head, like something malign trying to make its way out. Afterwards, her scalp would feel bruised, sore to the touch.

It wasn't the Pill, she'd stopped taking it long ago.

'It's your life,' said Eleanor brusquely. 'You live too much alone, with too many lousy memories. Move house. And I'll come and live with you.'

'What — ?'

Eleanor said shortly, 'That's my offer.'

And she didn't know what kind of offer it was, sexual or otherwise, committed or casual; she felt she couldn't tell that kind of thing any more, such instincts had gone.

'No,' she said, 'Not yet . . . I don't want to make any changes yet . . .'

'Why not?' said Eleanor sharply.

She couldn't say. It was a feeling of having unfinished business.

An amputated limb you still feel.

Time passed. Spring came, and then summer. 'Come away with me,' said Eleanor. 'Let's go walking in Wales.'

She declined.

'Come away with us,' said Eleanor another time, 'we're going biking in Norfolk.'

She shook her head.

'You deserve all you get,' said Eleanor, and went off all summer, biking and walking for ecology, and camping outside missile bases for peace.

Eleanor said, guessing: 'You make this bloody great mystical thing out of men.'

151

She replied, 'Are you sure that, by cutting them off, you don't do that too?'

They parted in hostility.

Eleanor stopped coming.

They met in the street, and Eleanor was polite, the worst insult she could give.

She was immobile. Seasons passed. The space-shuttle shot into the sky and buzzed its way back again, and governments proclaimed technological progress, and environmentalists decried the fact that the world was increasingly polluted, and all the while drought and famine spread across great stretches of the world. And feminists wrote explaining the connections between all of these things and everyone's private lives, and Bron, reasonably politicised now, as her feminist acquaintances would put it, believed it all in her heart and mind, and grieved. And yet, in her life, she could do nothing about it. In her life she was static and waiting, like a listener in the poem, trapped and silent in a house in a wood.

She had a dream which kept recurring: two severed hands lay on the turn-back of a sheet. She went to pick them up, to give them back to whoever they belonged to, and found she couldn't: the two severed hands were her own.

She interpreted it as meaning that, through lack of use, she had lost the power to do anything about the ills of the world.

She had never known herself as part of history. She had spent her time on the side-lines, laughing and spraying hair-dye at the ozone layer, or sitting weeping inside. She had come to live on a deeper darker current. And that current, even now, was failing. Her movements slowed. The moon rose in the sky, swelled and shrank, and though she bled with its flux, her white elastic mid-month flow of ovulation had ceased. Her body slowing down, fading, becoming insubstantial.

Dear Bron,
    Please come. Dad has tried to take his life. He's been in hospital in Leeds. He's out now, and as well as he can be. But please, please, come.
    Elspeth.

Emotional blackmail, Eleanor would call it.
    Eleanor's voice in her head, a potent echo left behind. But other echoes, more potent for being fainter, like ghostly magnetic recordings in old walls.
    Don't leave me.
    Who said that? No one. He hadn't said it, too angry, too proud, they were the words you didn't say.
    She hadn't said them. 'Look after your mother,' he had said, her father, about to start the engine and drive away for ever, and before she said anything the car slid away, she'd been holding the handle, and it literally slid right out of her hand.

She packed a hold-all; she threw some watercolours and brushes in the leather case. A current pulled her along the metal railway, like the magnetic pull of the moon.

36

He said, 'Please stay, at least till Elspeth gets back.'

She said, worrying a little, 'Well . . . all right, till Elspeth gets back,' and she thought how odd it was of Elspeth, after such a desperate note, written from here, to nip off, as he'd put it, even before her arrival, to spend a few days with friends.

She picked up a cup and a spider fell out of it. It struck her that the house contained no evidence of his wife who had departed, as if she'd never existed at all . . .

But then the phone rang, and he jumped, as if back to life, and went quickly to answer it, and his voice coming through the open hall door was light and eager.

In the mote-filled kitchen, she sat and listened. He was inviting someone to dinner. Tonight. The dog, a scraggy collie slumped before the stove, opened one eye and caught hers, as if disturbed by her own alertness, and then sat up, staring towards the hall in quiet anticipation.

Dave came back. He was standing straight now, he rubbed his hands. He said, 'Guests for dinner! Friends of mine, a couple who live just up the road.'

He said, going into the scullery and flinging back the freezer-lid with a rattling thud, 'I know you'll like them.' His eyes glittered as he plunged his arms in, and all around him cold mist curled.

He took vegetables and a knife; he chopped vigorously, the metal flashed. He whistled, he put on pans and steam rose.

She was confused. She said, 'You seem a lot better.'

He stopped, knife poised. 'But of course! How could I be otherwise, now that you've come?'

Eleanor hissed: *Go on – now*!

But she didn't. Confused, she was watching and waiting for things to fall into place.

He said cheerily, 'Make a salad dressing, will you?'

And then suddenly serious, grabbing her arm and stopping her as she shook the ingredients: 'You know, all those times in that hotel, I longed for this. I always wanted to do everything with you. Not just make love, but all the real things too.'

And she saw the trap closing round her, and Eleanor said: *Go on*! but suddenly he looked down and said, 'Hey, you can't be thinking of making a dressing without garlic?', ridiculously eager, almost tetchy, and she was confused again, suspecting a tension he'd been managing until now to hide.

'No vampires surely,' she said lamely, trying to make a joke of it. She put the garlic in.

He said significantly, 'Well done.'

As if it was important.

And it seemed that it was: the quality of the food, the way they set the table. She simply didn't understand it, this obsession with the modes of living, when he'd only recently chosen to reject living at all.

She had to assume it was his only way of coping: concentrating on details because the general was too frightening.

155

37

Here is a scene two hours later:

Two artists – a bearded man in baggy corduroys and a woman with lank hair in a floppy floral dress drive in their battered old Volvo to visit their neighbour.

'My feminist friends,' is how he introduces them to her, as they bang the battered doors and come up the path, the man strolling up with one hand in a corduroy pocket, the other extended, and saying to her breezily, 'Hello, there!', the woman trailing behind.

They have contemporary ideas, they have no respect for outdated ideologies, and Dave's female lover, as he will tell her later, has been mistaken in thinking he'd have anything to do with people who'd be otherwise.

Indeed, these people are one step ahead of anyone in their thinking. This is how the conversation goes as they're seated round the table savouring Dave's curry:

'You call yourself a feminist?' asks Dave's female lover of his friend the male artist. She is merry, a little drunk, nervousness making her a little belligerent. 'Isn't the term anti-sexist, for men?'

The male artist smiles knowingly.

She flushes. She says in a rush, 'Well, in London they'd lynch you.'

There is a sudden flutter of discomfort round the table; but because the artists are so knowing, so one step ahead, it only lasts a brief moment and the atmosphere settles immediately to one of solidarity: a look is passed, from the male artist to the female, and the female artist smiles and drops her eyes in complicity, lank greasy strands of hair falling round her face. All of them are half-smiling, as at a long-standing joke. Dave as well.

Then the male artist explains: 'Feminism, sexism. They're just terms. With respect' (turning to Dave) 'we'd prefer not to use these phrases at all. Words, as you know, can be twisted to mean anything. Indeed,' (now looking at her intently) 'as you indicate yourself, in some circles these very words are being used to perpetuate the kind of gender divisions they were first employed to banish. No' – and here he puts his hand on the back of the woman's neck, and the woman, in response, compliantly smiles – 'No, rather than feminism we prefer to use the phrase *gender deconstruction*.'

He runs his hand up and down the woman's back. 'We are in the process of breaking down gender divisions, not building them. We carry this through in our work.'

He and the woman turn to look at each other and smile.

The newcomer asks, 'How?' and hiccups.

'We paint together. We make joint paintings.'

'What, on the same canvas?'

'Glass, actually, at the moment.' But he nods. He and the woman and Dave all smile. As if painting, he strokes the woman's back.

The woman has said not a thing.

When they'd gone she said to Dave, 'God, look how many bottles we've drunk.'

Dave replied, 'He's alcoholic. His wife went off and

157

left him, choosing, of all times, just after he was diag-
nosed. It meant he never recovered.'

He seemed excited by the evening. His face was
flushed, his lips were tight with a kind of animated
tension. He seemed obsessed by the evening's feminist
theme. He said, leading her up to bed, carrying the
brandy bottle, 'You know, I know I behaved badly to
you. Ringing you up like that, out of the blue, being
nasty about your paintings . . .'

She waited.

He said, 'It was wrong. It was a very male and wrong
way to behave. I was hurt, and in a typically horrible
male way I showed my hurt by being nasty.'

She said, confused, wanting to believe his present
declaration of new consciousness, but unable to trust
him, 'There was no reason, in any case, for you to feel
hurt.'

He said quickly, 'But there was. I was hurt that you'd
kept something so important as your truly original
talent to yourself. It was something I could have revelled
in, been proud of for you.'

She was surprised. She was tempted to be pleased.

He said, 'And also, bullying you about your husband.
Bullying you with facts and the letter of psychiatric law.
Ignoring the spirit of things. I had no right.'

He paused, sipping the brandy. 'I know that's typically male. It's the way we were brought up. It's the
way we were conditioned.'

She said, 'You mean the accursed voices of your
education.'

He paused. He smiled. He said superciliously, 'I think

158

you got that quote wrong. It's: *the voices of my accursed human education.*'

She didn't laugh, as she might. She was distracted, by something – a vibration; a sound, perhaps, just below the range of human hearing, like cats breathing on the landing, perhaps, or the echo of human footsteps on he stairs . . .

He said, rolling towards her, 'Do you know what I'd like to see you wearing? A crimson satin corset.'

It wasn't a joke.

She didn't come. But then, with him she never had. She sat up on her elbows thinking about it. She'd never faked, and yet he always seemed to take it for granted she came.

She said suddenly, faintly sarcastic, 'Did you come?'

And he said, 'Yes, didn't you feel it?' and she was amazed. By his assumption that her sensations would echo his automatically . . .

She got up and went to the sink to wash.

She rushed back. 'Christ, we must be mad! I've no contraception! I might easily be pregnant!'

He didn't move. He was smoking, leaning up on his elbows. He smiled, the faintest smile, as if he'd guessed it all along.

He said slowly, carefully, 'I would love to have a baby by you.'

Her heart slapped closed like a fist.

She said, 'Well, I bloody wouldn't.'

Something whispered – or did it? – beyond the gap in the door and out on the landing. Was she frightened, or was she merely in a panic about the possibility of pregnancy? At any rate her pulse fluttered.

'Look,' she said, doing it now, at last, sitting down on the bed beside him. 'I have to tell you, Dave, I'm not committing myself to you.'

He said nothing, his face was immobile. He took a drag on his fag. Whatever it was in the house seemed to scrabble, as if something was caught with soft battering wings.

At last he spoke. 'You noticed I lapsed on my Stop Smoking Campaign.'

Pause.

He stubbed his fag out. 'I can start again, now you're here.'

'Dave – '

'Come to bed,' he said, drawing her in, and whatever it was seemed to move, unlock itself, and flew out into the night. It called across the fields, a strange wild cry like that of an unknown bird.

'Feral cats,' he said, hearing it too. 'Bloody vicious. They can eat a domestic cat alive.'

He switched off the light. He said, out of the darkness, 'And the book. Now that you're here, at long last I will finish the book.'

All night long, whenever she turned, she hit his back like a solid cliff-face. Once, near dawn, outside on the hills, the strange creature called.

38

She'd had a dream in the night. She told him about it, sitting on a stool in the bathroom while he shaved. The door stood open, permanently wedged with a pile of old books and a large iron pot. Using the bathroom last night, she'd tried to shut it, and he'd called, laughing: 'Your Methodist upbringing's showing, don't be a prude.' All the doors in the house wedged open, or swinging back again when you tried to shut them, their catches long since worn smooth. As if the air in the house, though so still, were nevertheless buoyed with a pressure, some flagrancy of will that she, as he said, out of her background, did not know . . .

He shaved, fastidiously. He was meticulous in his personal hygiene. He had his own kind of prudery.

Urgently, she told him about the dream:

'I was on this bus, going somewhere, I don't know where – though in the dream of course I knew; we were nearly there. There was a church; it was getting dark; the spire rose up against a navy-blue sky. The bus began to slow.

'But on the journey I'd undone the laces of my shoes; I bent to do them and discovered they were unravelled, like embroidery-silks and shiny, and the more I tried to do them, the more they slipped and slithered out of my hands.

'The bus was stopping. I wouldn't make it, without the shoes I couldn't get off at all.'

She was relieved to have told it, to have wrapped its trembling void in the safety of words.

And shown him how she felt, she hoped.

He said nothing. He went on shaving, the little razor making self-satisfied rasps.

She said, 'Well?'

He turned to her, his eyes red and blank amidst the shaving-soap. Then he dipped his razor and flicked it. 'Well what?'

'Can you see what it means?'

He paused. He seemed amused. 'What do *you* think it means?'

She felt suddenly trapped. 'That there's something I can't sort out, some knot I can't tie. It's a feeling I've had for a long time. There's something I need to understand, but I'm not sure what it is.'

He resumed shaving, pulling his mouth down. 'People should never try to interpret their own dreams.'

She was stung.

He stopped again. 'Look.' Razor poised. 'It's obvious what it is. It's a dream about marriage.'

'What?'

'The knot represents marriage. Note the presence of the church. Silk, as well: that has wedding associations. Above all, shoes: surely you know that shoes are a traditional symbol of domesticity – the old woman who lived in one, shoes on the backs of wedding cars and stuck on the tops of wedding cakes. . . . No, I can see a simple interpretation: you are preparing yourself to accept the inevitability of stepping off your lonely life's journey and marrying me . . .'

The sun swelled in the room. Dust-motes sizzled.

He said, 'The fear in the dream reflects a real-life though unrealistic fear of doing so, understandable in view of what you've been through.'

She said, 'But I've never thought of the possibility of marrying you.'

'Well, dreams reveal the subconscious. Your subconscious is working through the problem your conscious refuses to admit.'

He was dabbing his face with a towel, he was moving away. She said, 'Look, Dave, you have to know you're quite wrong about this. I can't make you any permanent commitment . . .'

He didn't answer straightaway. His back was a wide wall. Then he turned. 'Believe me . . .' He seemed grave. 'Dreams, the subconscious . . . I know about these things.'

And that was when a pocket of air on the landing subsided, collapsed, and allowed a door to swing a little further: or was it her own chest starting and disturbing the molecules all around . . .?

In the evening Elspeth would arrive, driven by Clive who would be en route to other friends in the area.

There was a photo of Elspeth on the sideboard in the living-room: a wide-faced girl with an open expression, her fair hair flying wild.

She said, 'You know, she wrote to me once before, and I said I'd meet her, but she never turned up.'

She looked to see if he knew. He was looking at the photo, and then at her, and then back again, half-smiling. He said, 'You could be sisters,' and still half-smiling walked out of the room.

In the meantime, before the others arrived, they would go to Leeds.

He gave her the choice of staying in and working

while he went alone, though it was clear he really wanted her to come. She chose to go, because she didn't want to stay alone in the still breathless house.

He sped down the lanes, and then out onto the motorway. She watched his hands on the wheel, barely touching, massive hands now lightly, perfectly in control. He swung the car into Leeds, flicking his wrist and whirling them round into a multi-storey car-park. 'There!' he said lightly, and opened the car door.

The door banged against another parked at the side.

A driver inside had been sleeping: at the impact he woke. He looked around.

He opened up, slowly, and slowly, deliberately stood, and then, before her unbelieving eyes, took hold of his own door and viciously slammed it, over and over, like a tantruming three-year-old, into Dave's.

She wanted to laugh.

But then she noticed: Dave was leaning on the bonnet of his car, his eyes closed, sweat starting on his forehead.

The other man, petulant, sheepish now, was climbing back into his car, starting the engine. He began to back the vehicle away.

She said, 'What's wrong?'

Dave didn't move; as if the slightest effort would hurt.

At last he said, whispering: 'I wanted to kill him.'

It was hyperbole, surely, typical male violence-terminology.

But he caught her hand, and the sweat on his face poured in real rivulets. 'No. No, really. You don't understand. I really wanted to kill him. I could . . . . Remember, I was a soldier. It's how we were trained.'

39

They drove back. Ahead, over the hills, the sky was darkening with clouds. They turned into the lane and the light was yellow. Five o'clock. Two hours before Elspeth and Clive would arrive. He switched off the engine. There was silence. The bees had stopped droning. On the moor above, a line of sheep moved silently downwards seeking shelter before the rain.

Dave went inside. Since the incident in the car-park he'd spoken little, he'd been reticent, stiff.

She stood in the garden. A ripple of air caught the lower branches of a sycamore, a little whirlpool, like the central starting-point of the storm. But then it sank, and all was still. On the hill, the sheep reached a gateway and huddled.

Inside he was unpacking, preparing to cook. She went upstairs with the inks she'd bought and sat and worked on some sketches.

She kept thinking she heard movements, as though, without her realising it, they'd arrived.

When they did arrive there was no mistaking it: a car roaring up the lane and into the drive, and then a commotion of girlish squeals, Clive's voice, then Dave's, and a clatter of running feet on the yard, movement so energetic that by the time she stood and looked out Clive was already going back to the car, a convertible with the hood down, and the others had disappeared. Both the car doors hung wide, as though a whole party, rather than two people, had disgorged.

Now, however, all went quiet. She went down.

In the kitchen, Clive was standing nearest with his

back to her, opening a bottle of wine. Beyond, Dave and his daughter were clasping each other tight. None of them noticed her arrive. She stood in the doorway. The only sound was the corkscrew clicking.

Her foot scraped; no one seemed to hear. She coughed; she said, 'Hi.' Was she invisible, her voice inaudible to the human ear? But then all of them together looked up, almost as if tacitly agreeing that the moment had come to acknowledge her; it was like a dance when the music starts up again; sound and movement seemed suddenly to re-enter the room, Clive's elbow pumped more vigorously as he called to her, 'Hi there!' and Dave and Elspeth swept apart, and Elspeth said cheerily – indeed it seemed with great pleasure – 'Oh, *Hi!*'

As if, for a moment, time had stood still – for herself but not for them. As if her perceptions were disordered.

They sat eating Dave's ratatouille.

The evening was hot; hot for September. They'd opened a window, but from the outer darkness came no breeze, nothing tangible, just a sense of electric currents charging the air.

'Dad's a great cook,' said Elspeth, cheerily blithe, looking just like her cheery blithe photo, a cheery middle-class daughter who'd never known insecurity.

Something was wrong.

The air seemed to tilt; currents entered at odd angles.

'Ah, well,' said Clive, answering Elspeth. 'That's because he's an artist. Artists are always good cooks.'

She tensed. Amenable as he seemed now, she was afraid of this man, this authority on artists, who kept a check on them through computers, who through computers had watched her, preparing her a category even though she might be missing, keeping his finger on her back, pressing on a nerve.

But his tone was light, he seemed to mean no malice, to her or to anyone; they all seemed jolly, Dave as well, he had really cheered up; there they were, light and easy, as if nothing bad had ever happened, a happy party round the table, and it was only she who sat on edge like a maenad at the feast.

'Well, that figures,' said Elspeth. 'Dad was always great at cooking, and Mum was always lousy.'

The first mention of Dave's wife. She listened, waiting.

Clive laughed. 'Well, that just shows you how stupid traditional sex-roles can be.'

'Mind you,' said Dave. 'Amanda was the archetypal Dreadful Woman Driver. Sent to earth to set back women's equality fifty years in the matter of access to cars.'

He sniggered; they all sniggered; she shrank from their collective ridicule, and yet there was something almost like cloying love in their scorn.

She said suddenly: 'I thought you said she didn't drive.'

It was as though she had thrown a stone.

There was a pause. Dave said coldly, 'I never said that. I said it was best whenever possible not to let her.'

Clive and Elspeth sniggered again faintly, but there was an atmosphere of disapproval and offence, as if she'd breached their trust in trying to make out he had told her a lie.

She said, 'Well, anyway, I don't feel you can make any generalisations. I feel it's different for every artist; each artist has a different amount of creativity left over for other things . . .'

Dave interrupted her. His sudden viciousness, in spite of the knowledge that she was already out of favour, shocked her. He said, about her to the others, 'Note that.'

Then, turning to her: 'What do you mean, you "feel"? Are you expressing an opinion which is the result of logical thought; or are you simply uttering some kind of vague emotion? That's your trouble, you know: you are constantly confusing thought and feeling, messing up the former with the latter.'

What was going on?

She said wildly, 'No! As a matter of fact, it's not something I've thought out rationally, but I don't agree that makes it less valid. It's an intuition; I value intuition as a way of knowing things.'

There was a silence. Dave resumed eating. There was an air of heavy understanding, as though they'd heard it all before, and it was anyway beside the point.

Dave said, not unkindly now, 'You're a very emotional person.'

They all stared at her. Elspeth smiled at her indulgently.

And then, as though considering it time to dispense with such trivial matters, as though dismissing her, Clive said, 'I've bought the proofs of that paper, by the way, Dave,' and the talk after that was of books and, as in London, films and mutual friends, and Elspeth commented and laughed: 'Oh, yes, he bought me a teddy'; 'That's right – he sat me on his knee for the opening of the play', all smiling and shiny, not a girl who would brood or send a letter in desperation . . .

'We'll wash up,' she said quickly as they finished, meaning Elspeth and herself. She wanted to get her alone.

'Traditional sex-roles?' mocked Clive.

'Oh go on,' retorted Elspeth. 'We'll let you off for once, go and discuss your boring paper,' and helped them through with it and their brandy and coffee, making a parody of the little waitress woman.

She came back rushing, as if having got the coast clear at last.

'Bron! It's so wonderful you've come! The difference in Dad, it's just marvellous! Oh, I know he's going to get better altogether, now you're here!'

Did Elspeth think she had come here to stay?

'You know I'm going home tomorrow?'

Elspeth faltered.

And then here it was after all, the desperation, a white ripple of it flickering up in her amber eyes. 'Oh, Bron, you can't!'

'But I am. It's all agreed. I nearly went today.'

But of course it had been nothing so casual, there had never been any nearly about it.

'But Dad loves you!'

And now the wind got hold of the leaves, and away beyond the hill you could hear the storm imploding at its centre.

'I think he feels he needs me. I guess you feel he does too. But it's not the same as love. And no one should need another person that much.'

169

'What utter rubbish!' There was a shocking force in her voice. 'What utter rationalising rubbish! When you love someone the way Dad loves you, then of course it becomes a need! But it's nothing you can *help*!'

'But you can't help it either if you don't happen to need or love a person back.'

'But Bron, you do!'

The window banged, making them jump, and the light-bulb flickered. Elspeth's eyes were enormous, her hair wild, seeming on end. 'You do! Look how miserable you've been since you and Dad split up. Look how sad you are, and thin, it's so obvious you've been unhappy.'

'It's not as simple as you think. You've built up the wrong idea. . . . If you'd met me in London I – '

And just then the window slammed again and hard drops hit the glass like pebbles and Dave and Clive ran through with shouts, to put the hood up on Clive's car, and the dog barked, and the rain began to hiss like a chemical reaction.

She got up and shut the window.

The men came back and wiped their heads on towels, and commented tauntingly on the lack of progress with the washing-up, and went back into the lounge.

She sank to the table. 'Elspeth, look. It's not as simple as you think. My relationship with Dave has made too many people unhappy. Look at you: you had to leave university, you couldn't concentrate on your own life.'

Elspeth flashed: 'That's just not true! Don't you understand? It's since you've gone that we've all been miserable again. We were all so much happier when Dad had a relationship with you! All of us, even Mum,

170

because Dad was so much happier, and it lessened the strain between them. Of course, to begin with, we didn't know why it was – oh, don't look at me like that!'

She leaned forwards, her hands on the table. 'You think that because two people are married they'll be devastated by infidelity. It must be right what Dad says: your own terrible experience, your father just going off like that, has made you put too much store by faithfulness in marriage. I suppose, as he says, it's why you feel so guilty about it all when you just don't need to. Well, Mum and Dad always had a quite different attitude.'

She sat also, becoming contemplative, beginning to talk as if she were thinking aloud. 'They always both had affairs . . . and I always knew it, I think. . . . At any rate, I knew it for sure from about the age of thirteen. They didn't hide it, because they didn't feel there was anything to be ashamed of: there's no point in being ashamed of something you can't help – falling in love, or needing other people.'

It sounded so neat. She looked around, and out through the window to the rain-washed darkness, and thought of the lonely hills out there, unpeopled, devoid of others to give you support or friendship, or to fall in love with. . . .

Elspeth was saying: 'Mind you, years before Dad met you they'd decided to divorce; I guess they'd come to the conclusion that it was happening so often they really must be failing badly to satisfy each other. I guess I grew up, went through my teens with the acceptance of that. It was always on the horizon, but they never got around to it. Maybe because none of Dad's affairs ever made him happy either. We had some terrible times when they broke up. He always went through hell, always broke down completely . . .

'But then he met you. We had never seen him so buoyant, so full of life. And when he told her the reason, Mum couldn't help being glad, because now at long last Dad might be cured of his illness.'

'Illness?' What was this?

Elspeth looked amazed. 'Well, of course – Dad's depressive illness. The reason for all his breakdowns, all those times he's tried to take his life . . .'

40

All those scars, silver streaks across his body.

These, sustained by falling in a drugged daze off the bed and through a glass table; these, by walking through a sheet-glass hospital door.

He sat up naked in bed, tracing the history of each silver scar. The house was silent; the rain had stopped. Clive had driven off into the hissing rumbling night.

Every time, he had taken pills.

Was this the secret? The secret she'd been waiting for?

And yet she was confused. All along he'd been facing up to death, embracing it wilfully. But what about his inordinate fear of it . . . the desperate bid to stop smoking. . . . Don't joke about death, he had said. Once, telling him about her father, she'd laughed, 'Why don't they call it death insurance?', and he hadn't liked it at all. . . . She had said to him, earlier in the day, 'Do you know, all that time when we'd lost touch, I sometimes thought you must be dead.' And he'd bristled, his tone offended, he'd said, 'You must be joking, I'm a survivor.'

His face now had a look of peace. As if he too had been waiting for this, and now that it was done could relax.

The grand revelation. The consummation.

He bent to stub his cigarette out. In the lamplight, the scars gleamed like brocade. Silver stripes. Battle stripes. He moved towards her, sexually aroused.

And then she knew, she understood: the fear and the glorification were one, two sides of a coin rolled in a dangerous game.

She froze. He put his hand on her breast.

She said, 'No, remember, I have no contraception.'

He said, 'A baby by you would be lovely.'

By you, he said; not *with you*.

She backed away, she went off to the bathroom.

When she came back he was bent away from her over the bed. He straightened, holding something she could not see. He moved across to the door. In this house where the doors always swung open, he slid the lock across. He turned, and uncrumpled the thing he was holding. Crimson, sheeny, it fell in folds, with black flickings of lace. The satin corset.

He held it towards her, pushing the fantasy through the borders towards her. The sheeny lines tumbled sickly.

He said, 'See, thanks to you, I cut down and saved up.'

He said, 'You'll look a dish in it.'

(Once he'd said, 'You're a dish,' and she'd retorted, sarcastic: 'Not a tart?' and he laughed: 'What's the difference, they're both culinary terms.')

She shook her head.

'Aw, come on.'

He thought she was joking, playing a game; her mock-fright, as he saw it, aroused him.

She saw in horror how all along they'd been edging through the fantasy, each time pushing the boundary a little bit further, first a garter, then a black stocking; next suspenders: all for a bit of magic, a bit of conjurors' magic. But conjurors' magic was after all grounded in reality, conjurors were calculated, conjurors prepared tricks behind the scenes . . .

He'd written: *I'll prepare you a feast you won't be able to refuse . . .*

Black elastic snapping like schoolboys' rubber bands, black stockings painting out her legs. Her body cut up, crotch from legs, crotch from stomach and breasts. And now this.

She moved away. He pulled her arm. She was half-undressed already. He pushed it up against her, seeing what it looked like; she pushed it away.

He said, 'Aw, come on, you said you would!'

'I didn't, don't be silly.'

He went still. He said, ominously calm, 'What did you say?'

She said, half-laughing, half in fright, his fingers digging painfully into her arm, 'I said I didn't. It was a joke, you can't be serious!'

174

He went white around the lips; she knew then that he would not forgive her for this: for laughing at him.

He said viciously, 'What are you, a prude?' He jerked her arm roughly.

She cried, in agony, 'Leave me alone!'; he jerked again, she choked contemptuously, 'You bully!' and that was when his hand came flying like a planet out of the air towards her, larger than life.

She came to. He was lying above her. He was sobbing. His weight crushed her. It was dark in the room, the light-bulb seemed to have gone. She eased herself out, and allowing her, he rolled away. Her mouth was throbbing.

He sobbed, 'Forgive me, oh Bron, forgive me.' His hands were all over her, stroking over and over, as if trying to bring a dead body back to life. But she was alive; numb and throbbing, but solid and alive. She moved further away. He groaned. He said, 'Please forgive me.'

The storm growled somewhere to the south.

'Don't leave me,' he said, saying it now.

She sat apart, closed tight inside her body.

He said after a while, 'Please. I need help. I think I may be alcoholic.'

She packed herself even tighter.

There was a peace in the air, as though, having moved inwards, her heart had relieved the molecules around.

Even so, the lightning still flickered, a film slipping backwards at the end of the reel.

Slowly she realised that from somewhere else in the house also was coming the sound of sobbing.

175

He jumped up. 'Elspeth.' He pulled on his clothes. He ran.

Slowly she got to her feet. She felt giddy. Her face was throbbing more painfully now, and she had a headache on one side.

There was a strange light in the room, and everything had a sharpness. Of course, it was the moon: she'd lived so long in the all-night sulphur lighting of the city it took her by surprise. Sharper almost than daylight; inking everything round with black lines.

Through the sharp moonlit landscape she made her way to the mirror. She could see that her mouth was bleeding. She could feel now that one of her teeth was loose.

Bravery, cowardice; these were relative states: what she did from now on would be neither brave nor cowardly. Dread or hope had gone from her. Anything might happen to her, but it didn't matter as long as it was true to what she could see.

41

The sobbing upstairs had stopped. The house was silent. There was a faint smell of burning, as if the storm had actually singed the air. She went downstairs in the moonshine, moving through the house without aid of human light.

In the kitchen stove cinders flickered, about to go out, for once left to go out. The dog shifted, eyed her.

She went outside. The smell of singeing was in the wind. Somewhere, out of view, maybe lightning had struck. She looked back at the house. One square of light only: that of Elspeth's room.

She went back in.

He came downstairs. He said, 'She's OK now, she'll sleep.'

She didn't ask what had been wrong. She had stepped away from the treacherous leaden power of words. She merely watched, sensing how, in the moonlight, her own eyes glittered. He turned, he went back upstairs. Still neither of them had turned on the light. She took some coats off the hooks and wrapped them about her and slept in the lounge on the settee.

In the morning he woke her rattling the stove and making tea. She turned to see him through the open doorway, and her face caught on the arm of the settee, making her wince. He sat, elbows on the kitchen table, smoking and sipping his tea. Eventually he rose and opened up the back door and took the dog outside.

She got up stiffly. Through the window, she could see him going off down the lane, the dog at his heels. She poured two mugs of tea and took them upstairs.

Elspeth's door was ajar. She knocked. There was silence. She pushed the door in.

Elspeth lay, her eyes wide, watching as she entered. She sat up slowly.

'All right?' she asked, conscious of stiffness and pain on speaking, coming forward with the tea.

Elspeth stared. Her face was pasty, pudgey now, her hair snaggled in listless rats' tails. The ribbon on her

177

high-neck nightie looked sniffled-on and chewed. She reached out for the tea. She took a gulp, cupping with both hands, and her nose in the steam went red.

She said, 'Bron, don't go,' then quickly dropped her eyes. 'I know you and Dad had a fight.' She looked up, her eyes bright and wild now, she put down the tea and leaned forward and grabbed hold. 'But don't go! Please! Don't judge Dad on that, on one row, he's beside himself, he's in such a state, it's his illness, and the thought of losing you!' Her white face was pushed forward, she was starting to cry, her eyes reddening, she was spitting, there was food between her teeth. Her fingers dug.

It was ridiculous, it was confusing: a grown woman, as Elspeth in spite of her present appearance undoubtedly was, pasty-faced and sleepless, beside herself, it seemed, over the break-up between her father and his lover. What was going on?

Elspeth gargled: 'Oh, Bron, if he loses you, just think what he'll do to himself!'

So that was it. Elspeth would use her to keep him safe. She drew back.

'Elspeth. We can't go on propping him up in this way. Women can't go on doing it: standing between men and their own weakness or violence. It destroys us. Look at me' (pointing to her own face). 'Look at your mother – '

'My mother – ' Elspeth snarled, guttural, almost frightening ' – was *ill*! It was nothing to do with Dad, how dare you imply it was all his fault. And she turned her back on him, she did nothing for him, she always

178

turned away when he needed her most.' She gave a sob, a great gouge of sound.

'Perhaps she had to. She probably knew that in the end we can't protect men from themselves, however hard we try. Look at you . . .'

And she looked at her, bedraggled in a tangled mass of sheets. And then noticed a small brown bottle beside the bed.

'What are those?'

Quiet, defensive: 'They're my pills.'

Valium.

'Do you take them all the time?'

'When I get in a state.'

When things get frightening, when you crumple, don't make your exams or turn up to meetings in London . . .

Elspeth looked up. 'Like last night.' She was defiant now, even a little smug. 'Dad made me take some. You see, he cares. He looks after me, he just isn't the kind of man you think.' She was rising to anger.

'Elspeth,' she said urgently, sitting down again beside her, holding her arms now, 'you can't go on like this. Can't you see what it's doing to you? You have to stop letting him depend on you.'

Elspeth screamed, a great gush of high-pitched rage, and jerked, flinging away the restraining arm so that it shot back upwards and knocked the loosened tooth. Elspeth jumped back in the bed on her haunches, her nightie riding up, the sinews of her inner thighs stretched; she screamed: 'How dare you! How dare you suggest my father is the cause of all my problems! It's what you were doing last night, isn't it, implying Dad is the cause of the problems of all of us – it's so unfair;

179

Dad has cared for both Mum and me in our difficulties when really he needed to be looked after himself, it's *we* who have been depending on *him*! You make him sound like a monster, and he's the most gentle and kind and loving man in the world. I love him so much! There must be something wrong with you.'

'Fear of men.' The voice came from the doorway: Dave's.

He was massive, immobile, a solid cliff, his face closed. She was afraid.

But Elspeth, on the contrary, scrabbled up, in relief, and sprang across the room to him, the child running for succour to the parent, and clung to his side. He put his arm around her shoulders.

'A father-deprived adolescence,' he said.

They were looking at her. He went on: 'Inducing a sense of men as the Unknown. Leading to sexual inexperience, a certain fear of experience generally, leading to self-incarceration. This inevitably led to a disastrous marriage, though indeed a marriage that served a certain purpose in providing a world of masks and disguises in which the man-woman relationship didn't need to be fully confronted.'

He put his hand on the door-frame, warming to his theme. Elspeth linked his other arm, almost cosily. 'A personality thus castrated loses its cohesiveness. Phantasies of breaking apart occur, unusually manifest in this particular case in a series of paintings she did at one time. . . .'

He tucked Elspeth beneath his shoulder. 'In short, neurotic illness.'

She laughed. As she opened her mouth, the tooth dropped out. Falling apart.

A look passed between Dave and Elspeth: significant. Something understood, something rehearsed.

Dave nodded. Elspeth began moving sideways like a crab, circling her. Elspeth jerked, and in response, involuntarily, she flinched; Dave said, 'Quick, get between her and the window!' and Elspeth darted round.

Of course. They thought she was mad. Standing there toothless and grinning, all her words turned to ashes and broken falling teeth, like the madwoman in the attic, or mad mistress on the landing, crashing about, scaring children. Whatever she did they'd call her mad, cruel or mad and what was the difference, mad because she loved or mad because she didn't.

Dave began moving about the room, picking up objects, a small mirror, a nail-scissors, a glass tumbler, things she could hurt herself with. . . . Her mind tipped. Perhaps, to have ended in this situation, she really was mad. . . .

42

The ambulance drove away down the lane.

Clive shut the yard gate. She was alone with him now. He walked straight past her, his face grim.

Of course, he blamed her.

Elspeth slumped across her bed, the bottle of pills empty, lidless on the floor.

In gathering up the instruments of self-destruction, Dave had failed to move the pills. Perhaps because she herself had moved suddenly forward and said quietly, at last saying it, at last able to say it: 'I'm leaving.'

He had moved to stop her. Brute force, enormous hands. *I want to level*, he had said. He could level her, he could kill with a blow.

But she had gone from her body. They could not affect her now, whatever they struggled to do to it, save it or kill it. Floating, bodiless, she glared.

He sensed; he gave.

She walked away, out of the room.

Back in the room, Elspeth suddenly wailed.

She'd packed her things. She'd gone downstairs. In a while, he came down. He sat apart, leaving her alone.

She would walk the two miles to the station.

She went to get her jacket and through the window she saw Clive returning, his car nosing into the yard.

It was Clive who found Elspeth. He'd seemed to know. 'What's going on?' he asked, entering the kitchen, looking from one to the other, clicking in, like someone turning on the TV into a film he knows well.

And then he rushed up the stairs, and then was calling instructions and trying to make Elspeth sick.

And Dave was moving towards the phone and dialling, like someone in a dream, a recurring dream or an old familiar film.

Of course they blamed her.

182

They blamed her for everything:

'I must talk to you about Amanda,' Clive had said significantly, touching Dave's elbow as he clambered behind the stretcher into the ambulance, looking pointedly past her as she stood at the side. 'She's in a state. She seems to be only just coping . . . you should see the mess she lives in . . .'

'She was always lousy at housework,' was all Dave said.

But there was a tacit acknowledgment, after all their denials: of herself as usurper, spoiler, bringer of ashes.

Clive the healer, the friend in bad times, opened up his briefcase now, gathering his things, and slipped the proofs of his paper inside.

She had read it. It had been lying on Dave's desk as she packed. The title had caught her eye. RATIONALITY IN ART – MINOR ART AS MANIFESTATION OF NEUROTIC ILLNESS: A CASE-HISTORY.

She'd scanned the print: . . . *deprivation of father in early adolescence . . . loss of psychic cohesion . . . phantasies of breaking up . . . manifest here in the violent portrayal of disembodied human organs . . .*

The artist, ostensibly in deference to her dignity, unnamed.

Unnamed, made invisible, pushed back to the sink, the messy flat, however lousy she might be at housework, to the ashes of the stove . . .

Dave had said to Clive, the night before, looking up from these proofs: 'I have a book that I've been working on, on and off, over the years . . .'

She'd searched, she'd found it in his desk-drawer. As

she opened up the drawer, a sickly-perfume smell of old confectionery was released. The chocolate papers were there, in an old plastic bag along with the wrapper from the aspirin and a styrofoam cup with a piece bitten out of it.

Now the manuscript was shut in her leather case.

She said, 'I'm going,' and he nodded sternly and she walked out into the hall.

The lounge door hung open, the purple curtains that Amanda must have made in the end after all, hanging in the sunshine. Something moved.

She stood still. In a tube of light near the window, something was turning. Motes of dust, the molecules arranging themselves; a patch of colour assembling; a woman's shape, so for a moment she thought Amanda had been there in the house all along, but no, there was no substance: the shape changed; she saw her mother, she saw her father's old lover.

And then the apparition dissolved. Nothing there but sunshine, and the dust-motes dancing. And the air was light, fresh after the storm, and she stepped out into it and began to walk the two miles to the town.

43

Of course afterwards, I felt less sure. Reaching the town I started looking backwards, expecting to see Clive's car coming down the road behind me, midnight striking for Cinderella, his silence as I left simply grim confidence of easily overtaking me. The ends of stories do not come so easily, their beginnings wash over them, old patterns flicker, it is not easy to stop fearing the power of men.

My limbs ached; I had begun to settle back inside my own body. My arms, I noticed, putting down my bags in the station foyer and pulling up my sleeves, were bruised. It is in our bodies we are vulnerable after all.

I bought a ticket to London. The ticket-clerk gave me a look that was at once an imposition and a dismissal. He noticed me, I was noticeable, with my swollen bruised face; at the same time he didn't want to notice me: I was undesirable, a tramp, a hag. He watched me covertly as I walked away, and then resolutely turned his shoulder in my direction.

I sat on a bench on the platform. I started shivering uncontrollably, wondering for a moment if the weather had changed, but feeling the sun strike hot on my skin. I eyed the entrance. Any minute now, I thought, Clive might appear there.

I thought of Elspeth, crouched and snarling on her bed in her passionate allegiance, snarling face, snarling crotch; I felt frightened and alone, I did not believe in the power of women to stop lashing at each other from under the protection of men.

I saw them all in allegiance against me for ever: Clive and Dave and Elspeth, and probably Amanda. Who else? Which of their contacts, which publishers, which people with power in the world of art and illustration, any world in which I might try to gain some dignity, the old net, old liaisons criss-crossing the present, old stories encroaching on the new.

185

And there was I, alone in the world, a drifter, with a past that was only private, I was nothing in the face of it.

At the edge of my consciousness, out there in the world where people coped, made their mark and spoke in voices that were heard, the railway loudspeaker boomed: *The train about to arrive at platform two is the four-forty-five to Scarborough*, and to the west of the station that train crawled, a yellow-and-blue caterpillar entering my field of vision.

The power of computers against me: Clive with his finger on the button, conjuring up my life behind my back, rubbing the lamp and capturing my soul. The flick of a button, the turn of a dial. The power to summon, the power to intercept. Across at the other platform, the train slid in. They could have someone waiting for my train by the time I got to London.

The train had stopped, the doors were banging.

That was it. I could go where they couldn't find me. I got up, I crossed the bridge, I ran, my feet slamming on the empty platform, there was no one left, the train was about to leave again, I grabbed a door and got inside the Scarborough train.

The train slipped, began to move. But someone else, further down, got on behind me. There was no escape from the fear. I shrivelled up inside my skin.

44

And arriving here at dusk, sensing shadows dart behind me, walking beneath satellites capable of tracing a figure moving down a street, I knocked on your door.

And down you came, in your odd floral pinafore, like a disguise, and your face like a mask, and I was afraid.

And in I stepped, and you closed the door. And away across the country my council flat would be boarded up, and the computer print-out of the state of my bank account would stop like a heart.

But you, noticing my arms all wealed and mottled, said, 'A nettle-rash without nettles means a secret without telling.'

And you'd knocked the case, containing the manuscript, out from under the bed:

Some of it is old, some more recent. Yellowed pages and newer whiter ones rearranged with scissors and paste.

She was an illustrator of mediocre talent. I met her at a literary party. I looked up and saw her. She was the one I had been waiting for all my life. She looked down, she had seen me watching. She knew. She was dressed entirely in black.

All my life I had been looking. I was cautious. Many times had I believed, wrongly, that that moment had come.

We walked through Chelsea. On the corner of Cheyne Walk I looked up. The sun flashed orange on the window of the flat where all those years ago I'd lived with Brenda. Like a signal. For a moment I thought I saw, in that window, a pale face. Brenda's ghost, looking out, taunting, as women in the end always do.

'I used to live up there,' I said to the soft wispy woman at my side, and the face above flashed, a flash of jealousy, and then faded, a wistful shade.

I had exorcised Brenda.

We walked on.

I bought her chocolates.

I was testing it out, the strength of the exorcism. I went to Tyler's, where once long ago I'd first caught sight of Brenda behind the glittering sweet-smelling counter. Here I bought chocolates for Bron. Here, over the counter where Brenda's arm had once reached, handing me chocolates years before, her white white arm that had arrested me in mid-exchange and caused me to look up and meet her eyes.

Sweet Brenda among the sweets, dressed all in white.

We had arranged to meet.

I began to dread that she wouldn't turn up. She would be just like the others, who all laughed and promised everything, but in the end betrayed.

The clock where I stood had already struck six. But then she came, round the corner, out of breath, her soft brown hair in a cloud. After all, she had not betrayed me.

But the seed of doubt had been sown. Had she done it on purpose, to tease, to warn, to wield her wily female powers? At best, she'd shown a carelessness, a disregard which is the unholy legacy of women. . . .

We went for wine. Another test.

'Here's a wine-shop,' she said, and for a moment I thought, panicking, that the shop-front had been altered, the past obliterated before I could perform my exorcism.

But this shop was new. The old one was still there, several doors down, where once, before going to the hotel, Vicky and I had bought wine.

I said, 'What wine do you like?'

She replied, 'White.'

She was touching in her naivety. My doubts dissolved.

I shut the hotel-room door. I could feel myself sweating. Would it work? This room, this purple room, number 3, where the others, Vicky, and before her Rebecca, had rocked me in their arms only to walk away?

I turned. She was lying on the bed. She was laughing. Temptress, flaunting. Her laughter merged with the mocking laughter of all the others. My manhood failed me.

She was not on the Pill. I was to be reduced to the ugly charade of a rubber sheath. She lay back, her hands tauntingly behind her head, and laughed.

But then she melted. She leaned forward and put her arms about me, like a mother, a soft wispy little mother, and whispered, 'It doesn't matter,' and I knew that my fears, my dread were without foundation: this woman was not like the others, she was giving, she was receptive, she wouldn't deny my virility, my seed, she cared enough to bear my child.

Although later, she went on the Pill. She withdrew that generosity, that openness of possibility. She came to our encounters merely for the satisfaction of her lust. Like all the others, whose rubber caps had lain like cold dead fish-eyes on bedside cabinets and wash-basin shelves, a cold dead stare that said: Come so far, but no further. Symbols of women's freedom to sleep with other men . . .

Depression overtook me, I began to fade.

I tried to hold on. I took the pieces of our encounters – chocolate papers, aspirin wraps, bits of styrofoam cups – I tried to keep it all alive.

I wrapped them all up in the bag from Tyler's, that Brenda had handed me that first time so many years ago. . . .

But the spell was breaking. We went back to the hotel, the birth-pill streaming in her veins, and the room, our special room, number 3, was not available. The pattern shifting: all the furnishings the same, purple bedspread, purple carpet, grey lace curtains, but outside the door the well of the stairs. . . . If I didn't keep control of the pattern of things, I knew they would spin off in frightening ways. . . . She would turn out to be no different from the rest.

Brenda was a virgin.

We put down towels. She cried. I flung the towels

in the sink, shock-red with blood. Even in innocence, especially in innocence, there is always pain, there is always blood. Innocence or profanity, it always ends in blood.

Vicky. I met Vicky at someone else's wedding. One white thigh exposed. She wore a deep-crimson dress with a slit right up the side. In the midst of the virginal wedding, it was her profanity that attracted me.

It was the seed, did I but know it, of the squalor that would destroy it all in the end. . . .

There is no exorcism. Each one, brought to exorcise the others, in fact conjures them up, calls them up, laughing; they are all in league with one another, they have known each other always, since the dawn of time. And they line themselves up and down the corridors of my past, treacherously smiling, and in my hour of need they gather round my bed. But it is to mock me they have come, in their black, in their white, in their throbbing gleaming crimson, Rebecca and Amanda and all the others, sweet Brenda turned to ice, Vicky laughing with the callous hatred of the whore. And as they mock, their masks, their disguises, their make-up fall away and the truth is revealed: the laughter is the mocking of empty skulls. . . .

And this one. The one in black. She is no different from the others. Oh, but she is. She is the worst.

I made a discovery. My love had a past she had carefully concealed. Amazingly, oh, devastatingly, this soft little woman, seeming so full of warmth and life, I discovered to be a woman who had tricked her

way into the art world through a series of manipu-
lations and disguises, and, though it grieves me to say
it, sexual wiles.

She was the Shrouded One. The one that all my
life, in fear and trembling, I have been waiting for:
The Faceless One.

She comes now, to my bedside, stepping forward
from the rest. She is the one who promised most and
gave least, who made the greatest betrayal. Her black
gown rustles.

She holds out her hand. Her left hand, her fatal
flaw. She hands me the pills.

She is the one whose temptation will finally enthrall
me.

Make a woman your murderer, and you justify her
death.

Shoot, I said, wanting him to tell me.

Our fate seems sealed by the spells the men have been
weaving. We may go to the ball, in our black, in our
white, our crimson satin with lace, but we will all be
ugly sisters in the ashes in the end. Dismembered,
chopped, as we have been in their minds all along,
trussed in black elastic, reduced to an arm or leg, one
white arm, one white smooth thigh, one left hand, a
headless body floating in the Thames. Or to relics: bits

of paper, plastic cups or plastic bags, packed one inside the other, stacked one inside each other like Russian dolls, fixed, like paper princesses in a scrap-book.

But I have colluded. Cutting out my paper princesses, sticking them down, pulling my hat down, saying nothing. I have colluded in my fate.

45

But then: is this my fate? Is it *fate*? A run-down house in a tatty northern seaside town? Or can I choose? Do I choose it, embrace it?

You commented on my rash. You said it meant a secret story. You leaned back, settling down to listen. Beneath the pinny, your body settled: not wrapped away for ever, but living and breathing. I looked through your make-up and saw a look of friendly interest. And you told me your name: Stella.

I stopped perceiving you through my fears.

And you took me down to your room, and there a baby was bouncing up and down in his cot, and so I knew that the noise I'd heard in the night was no ghost, no intruder, but his simple cry of hunger, which I had been perceiving through my fear.

I am culpable of the same sin, the same mechanism as he: I told you my story, and patterns flickered: male bodies leaping one-handed over walls, down from balconies, over the bonnets of cars, emerging from archways. I did the same, I imposed them one on the other, and cut them up, reduced them to one recurring slim ankle or wrist, stuffed one inside another in an old leather case.

The story runs, an old film flicking, new images and events negative repetitions of the old.

But the telling of the story moves the story on, and gives it new meanings, reveals secret stories within:

I walked away from Elspeth's bedroom. I'd said quietly, 'I'm leaving.' And Elspeth had wailed and flung herself across the bed.

I reached the top of the stairs. I turned.

All the doors in that house wide open, each room leading one to another, the life of each room running into the next. Sun streaming through the doorways onto the landing. Straight ahead, the view into Elspeth's room framed. And Elspeth's arms, white and thin, exposed where the nightie-sleeves had fallen back, flung around Dave. His face was buried in her neck. They moaned. They clapsed, with the helplessness of desperate lovers.

A listener, watching on the stair of that memory, I understand:

This is why I was summoned. This is why I was needed: to sweep Elspeth from the ashes. To take her place. To be Fairy Godmother, to set her free and allow her at long last to go to the Ball.

46

And yet read on; read his manuscript and see what it reveals:

There is a point where one needs to give up, give in, in order to obliterate pain.

Amanda was away doing some reading for some Women's Institute somewhere, playing at being a poet as usual, and would not be back till late. Elspeth was spending the night with a schoolfriend.

I was alone with my darkness. I could perform my task without interruption, and my purpose would be complete before anyone returned.

I turned in the doorway on my way out of the kitchen, taking one last look at the familiar scene, already gathering itself now into unfamiliarity, the walls closing, the red of the tiles concentrating. The dog sat up, alert, fixing me. 'Sit boy,' I said, and he sank, his chin on his paws, his eyes dark pools, looking at me once, and then staring forlornly ahead. He knew, he always does. A coal slipped in the stove. In the morning there would be cold ashes, no one would have replenished the fire.

I closed the door. I went into the hall. I walked towards the old clock hanging on the wall. I opened its casing. Inside, the bottle of whisky bought for me once, long ago, by Sylvia. 'Something for you,' they always whispered, smiling, giving me brandy, or whisky, or cigarettes, for Christmas, for my birthday. Something to rot your guts with, something to warm the cockles of your heart.

I take it out and close the casing with a little click, the last click. I cradle the bottle and slowly climb the stairs.

I hear a rustle on the landing. I know she is there.

I place the bottle on my bedside table. The glass is ready, the round brandy-glass, for cradling, for savouring. Also on the table are the pills. I unscrew the bottle. I put the pills on the table one by one. I group them in threes: ten little groups of three, like ten bright yellow flowers. I pour the whisky. It gurgles, like a brown peaty spring, like the earth itself giving forth its dank life; liquor of life, its name means: *usque baugh*.

I sit. I take a sip, and swirl the liquor on my tongue. A tang of peat, the years' decay compacted, a whiff of woodsmoke and fire, something to warm the black cockles of my heart. I place a pill on my tongue. I swallow.

Slowly, slowly does it.

I hear her move outside the door. She is coming. She will come. Another sip, another pill.

Slowly, slowly, the room begins to tip. There are five bright yellow flowers left.

There is a rustle. She has entered the room.

I fall back, I feel myself slip. The glass drops from my hand.

And she is there. She has come. She leans above me, the one in black, the Shrouded One. And I know that within that black hood she smiles.

'Come,' she whispers, holding out to me the rest of the pills, all of them, altogether, wanting me to gorge them now, with the unbridled appetite of women. 'Come,' leaning above me, coming closer, approaching the final consummation, climbing in beside me and drawing me down into the warmth of the final black womb. . . .

To give up, to give in. To relinquish the power that is too much to bear, that denies and destroys. To go away, to shuffle off the shoes of an unholy power.

But for this (slowly, slowly, one pill at a time, and five little yellow flower-groups only):

To come back.

To be saved. To sit afterwards in the sun with one's skin smoothed and clear, one's hands curling like a baby's on nursery-clean linen.

To be reborn.

But read on:

I woke. Pulled up against my will through sticky quicksands to a world of grey, of brutal metal and ice-cold lino, and the white inhumanity of the hospital gown.

A world empty of Vicky.

Walk, they say: move your legs, and they move them, push and pull you along the grey slippy spaces between the beds, forcing you back to a life you cannot bear to live.

They diagnose a condition. They call it something: depression, paranoia. . . . They do not call it sorrow.

Sorrow. We are all dying of sorrow, hobbling, unbalanced, one shoe off, one shoe on, one foot in the grave. We cannot be reborn, or balanced or whole, in a world where there is the violence of a power that denies.

It is not death we fear – although we think it is – so much as the violence in our lives.

But we sprout again, all of us: we jump from corners, out of archways, if not in our own bodies, then in those of others; we spill from cases, we are mad housewives in the ashes and turn out to be poets. This is the hope and the dread that has been moving the story all along.

Let us walk on this tatty northern prom. You and I, Stella, with your child, now that he is walking, let's hold his hands, one each side; let's cling together in the wind and the flying plastic bags and bottles.

Let's not be too afraid that the sea is radioactive, but let's also take account of the fact that it might be: not too much dread, not too much hope, not too much fantasy, not too much faith in slippery fact, let's keep a balance.

Let's swing the child and give him a good time. He doesn't know his father; let's hope it doesn't matter, and let's hope that if he did it wouldn't matter either. Let's hope he's just himself, he has no pattern of silence and power to retrace. Let's hope the future's open, let's hope it is a place where we don't need fairy godmothers.

Let's buy us all a lolly.

Says Bron.

We are coming back from the beach – I, Stella, with Bron: the two of us swinging my three-year-old child.

The wind batters us apart and he laughs, and so do we; our shrieks are snatched from us, we exult, shrieking again. Our words no longer feel wasted, we have each other to tell our stories, we scatter our calls like seeds into the buffeting, folding air.

Bron turns; I can't hear what she's saying, but from the movement of her lips I know: Let's run, she is saying, and we do, she picks him up and we run as best we can. And the sand blows against our legs, pricking, making us know the shape of them, making us know we are alive, grains shifting from the sand-dunes, the land changing its shape, and up above, the white crescent of moon a tiny new root in the afternoon sky.

Out of breath, we reach home.

As we're pulling off our coats, our other housemate appears on the stairs.

'Bron,' she calls quietly, a warning. 'There's a man here. He says he's been looking for you. He's waiting in the kitchen upstairs.'

Bron stands quite still.

Ex-lover, husband, father; Holy Trinity, unholy.

Myself, I feel afraid.

But then she gives me a brief straight look, and goes on up the stairs. She's not afraid. Whoever it is, there'll be nothing holy nor unholy, no mystique, in the sight of this man's face.